Bar Harbor Nights

A Mount Desert Island Series

Katie Winters

Chapter One

Angie stood in the center of Bar Harbor's Main Street with her arms wrapped around a thick paper bag filled with groceries. A watermelon surged through the bottom, threatening to break through. Still, she stood, captivated, as above her, two men on ladders stretched a large banner across Main Street, upon which someone had painted: GOD BLESS AMERICA.

It was the Fourth of July, and already after forty-plus years in the Midwest, Angie sensed that Bar Harbor residents did the Fourth of July a bit differently. Nonstop parties, sailing events, parades, and endless fireworks. It felt like the people of Bar Harbor had celebrated all weekend long already.

The men on ladders took several minutes to straighten everything, calling out across the street to one another. Neither seemed pleased with the other's work.

"Hi, Angie!" Heather Harvey appeared on the block. She wore enormous sunglasses, the kind suited for an actress, and a black dress that fluttered over her knees.

Angie's smile widened. This was her newly discovered

brother's girlfriend, a woman well-known in the children's fantasy book world. She was also a woman who'd been through significant heartaches, including the death of her dear husband, an oceanographer named Max. On top of it all, just last autumn, she'd discovered that she wasn't related to her sisters at all. The story was complex, involving an affair, an enormous lie, and an adoption that changed Heather's life forever. It was a miracle that Heather got out of bed every morning; despite all that, she blossomed with an effervescent joy that Angie only wished she could match.

Heather wrapped her arms around Angie and the bag of groceries, laughing. "I see you're out buying groceries before the rest of the town runs to the mini-market for last-minute supplies."

"I sure am. I had to beat the traffic."

Heather winced. "I wish I could be there today. Luke's just about as nervous as I've ever seen him."

Angie's smile fell. "I couldn't sleep last night."

"I imagine not." Heather tucked a dark curl behind her ear. "When was the last time you saw Wendy and Leo?"

"Sometime in May," Angie affirmed, remembering the anxious afternoon at her newly discovered mother's house in Boston, where she lived with her newly discovered older brother, Leo. Unlike herself and Luke, Leo had grown up with Wendy, as he'd been the oldest. Decades ago, Wendy had decided that he was the one she could keep after running away from an abusive husband. By contrast, Luke and Angie had gone to orphanages in the Cincinnati area— an act that had led Angie to a loving family and dropped Luke into a life of pain.

How could Luke ever forgive this woman for what she'd done? The question kept Angie up at night.

Naturally, when thoughts turned to her own life, to questions about why she hadn't been wanted, she shoved them away. Her adopted mother, Hannah (whom she'd named her daughter after), had been a godsend. And her father, Chester? He'd genuinely cared for her, even if he sometimes struggled to show it. His recent death had led her to all of this— this brand-new life in Bar Harbor. What a wild ride life was.

Angie straightened her sour grimace into a smile. "Oh, but you'll have such a blast with your girls on Martha's Vineyard."

Heather looked reticent. "We used to love going there, the four of us. Max, Kristine, Bella, and I."

Angie nodded. *What could she say?* Angie's husband had left her for a younger woman in their jazz band out in Chicago. That was a far cry from what Heather had experienced.

Still— they'd both experienced losses. The people you loved never lost their grip on your heart. Not fully, anyway.

"I better let you go to the airport," Angie began.

Heather blushed. She fell into Angie and gave her another hug, heaving a sigh. "Tell Luke I want him to call me the minute he has time to chat, okay?"

"Will do."

Angie walked back to her car, draped the grocery bag in the passenger seat, and drove out to Luke's place along the water. This was their agreed meet-up spot for Leo and Wendy. Luke stood out on the front porch in his traditional flannel, his eyes on the water of Frenchman Bay. In fact, Angie was halfway up the steps to his porch before he noticed her.

"Gosh, hi." He palmed the back of her neck as she gestured with the groceries. "Thank you for bringing those over. You really didn't have to."

But to Angie, the idea of Leo bringing their mother all the way to Bar Harbor was a cause for celebration— and fear. As a proper Midwestern girl (or, really, American), she planned to serve so many food options that nobody noticed how strained it was between them.

"Do you think she likes melon?" Angie asked, popping in through his screen door and positioning the groceries across his kitchen counter. "It looked so fresh today. So good. I have memories of Fourth of July watermelons from my childhood. Seems fitting."

Luke's eyes were hollow. Angie privately cursed herself, remembering that, actually, Luke probably hadn't had any sort of Fourth of July celebration during his childhood.

Luke entered the kitchen, closed the door, and checked his watch. "They should have been here about ten minutes ago."

Angie grimaced. "I'm sure they got caught in traffic or something."

"I guess we don't know if Leo's the type of guy who's good with directions or not," Luke pointed out. "He's basically a stranger."

Angie wanted to point out that, really, she and Luke were basically just "new friends" at this point. They'd just met earlier that year. They certainly didn't have a typical brother-sister relationship, although they fought to build one every day. She kept her mouth closed.

That moment, there was the sound of tires creaking over the gravel of Luke's driveway. Angie and Luke popped toward the front door, which Luke yanked open to reveal the rental vehicle that Leo had picked up from the airport. Leo lifted a hand in greeting. It was difficult to tell if the lifted hand was friendly or not.

Neither Luke nor Angie could comprehend what Leo felt about either of them. For decades, Leo hadn't known what his mother had done. He'd only lived and lived well, supporting his mother all he could, especially in the wake of her dementia diagnosis.

"Hi, there!" Angie's voice was overly bright and Midwestern. She couldn't help it. She jumped toward Leo as he got out of the car and gave him a hug. When he drew back, his cheeks were tinged red with embarrassment. Still, he looked almost pleased.

"Hi." Leo's eyes scanned across Luke's place and Frenchman Bay. "Good to be up here. It's so beautiful, isn't it?"

In the passenger seat, Wendy sat primly with her hands crossed over her lap. Angie braced herself. It normally took a good while to remind Wendy of who she and Luke were. Leo stepped around to the passenger side, opened the door, and spoke gently to their mother.

"Hi, Mom. We made it to Luke's house."

Wendy's voice rasped. "Who?"

"Your son. Your youngest son, Luke."

Wendy's face crumpled up. "That's right." It was difficult to tell if she actually remembered or just knew she needed to pretend. She placed her hand in Leo's and allowed herself to be helped up onto the gravel of the driveway. She then blinked up at the beautiful house curiously, her eyes stirring with questions.

"Hi, Mom." Angie's voice crackled as she stepped around to greet the older woman. It was a difficult thing to use that term, but she'd decided it was less confusing that way.

Wendy bristled and eyed Angie for a long moment, as though a stranger dared approach her and she wanted to fight them off. Angie stepped back, fearful. But after a long moment, Wendy turned her eyes toward Leo and simply said, "I think I'd like a glass of water."

Inside, Wendy sat at Luke's kitchen table as Angie poured a glass of water from the faucet. Leo and Luke did what all men always did: they discussed the route that Leo had driven from the airport and the spots that had filled up with Fourth of July traffic.

"Fourth of July being on a Monday means that's when the

traffic hits, I guess," Luke said nervously. "Everyone needs to get back home for tomorrow."

Angie placed the glass of water in front of her mother. Wendy wrapped her shaking hands around it and drank heartily, splashing a few droplets across her front. By the time she finished, her eyes shone brighter than ever.

"Gosh, I needed that," she said finally, sounding more like a healthy woman— a woman with full control of her mind.

Angie laughed. "I always get so dehydrated on planes." Not that she'd been on that many in her life.

"We had a great flight," Leo continued, sounding more optimistic. "They gave us free chocolate in honor of Fourth of July. If there's one thing Mom loves, it's sweets."

Wendy made a soft noise in the base of her throat, then tossed her head back, allowing laughter to flow out of her beautifully, like music. It was a staggering difference from the woman they'd just experienced back in the car.

"I always thought of Halloween as a time for Leo to go out hunting for candy for me," Wendy said, winking at Angie.

The corners of Angie's lips quivered into a smile. She glanced at Luke, who seemed similarly heartened. *Could they actually find a way to have real fun on this trip? Could they actually bond with their mother and brother the way they dreamed?*

Angie explained that she had a whole list of fixings for a hearty lunch. "After that, we thought we could head downtown for the Fourth of July Parade. Apparently, they hold one every year, and the entire town comes out for it." She leaned toward her mother to whisper, "You wouldn't believe this small town, Mom. After living in Chicago for my entire adult life, it's miraculous what it means to live alongside people who actually remember your name and care about what you've been up to."

Wendy nodded as though she understood, although it wasn't clear that she did. Angie's heart dropped a tiny bit as she scolded herself. *You can't just build a mother-daughter relationship out of nowhere, no matter how hard you want it. Give it time. Let her give you what she can.*

As Leo and Luke filled the space with continued conversation about the weather, baseball, and Leo's children back in Boston, Angie set to work slicing watermelon with a large, sharp chef's knife. She complimented it, to which Luke just said: "Come on, Ang. I'm a chef!" To this, she teased, "Last I heard, you were just a sous chef." To this, he stuck his tongue out playfully— something a little brother might have done to his older sister. Angie's heart ballooned.

The previous evening, Angie and her daughter, Hannah, had peeled and boiled potatoes, stirring them into a mustard-based potato salad. Now, Angie placed the potato salad in a large blue bowl with a big spoon for serving. She then sliced the fresh bread she'd grabbed from the bakery that was attached to the grocery store and set to work on making sandwiches with cold cuts and thick, delicious slabs of American cheese.

In her mind, it was the perfect Fourth of July lunch— before the real festivities began.

The four of them sat around Luke's kitchen table and ate. Through the open windows of Luke's kitchen, you could hear the roar of Frenchman Bay outside, frothing against the coastal rocks. Wendy ate slowly yet consistently, complimenting the freshness of the cold cuts and the crunch of the homemade bread.

"I used to make my own, you know," she told Angie. "That was back when it was a whole lot cheaper to just do everything yourself."

"I would love to learn how to do that," Angie breathed, suddenly drawing up an image of herself and Wendy, kneading dough and gossiping together.

That, too, would probably remain a fantasy. But a girl could dream.

After lunch, Angie packed up the leftovers and lodged them in Luke's fridge. Gosh, it felt nice to take care of these people, a family she'd never known. After Hannah had disappeared from her life and her husband had left her, Angie had felt a horrific emptiness, a knowledge that nobody really needed her anymore.

Now, she was needed more than ever.

* * *

It was decided that they drive Leo's rental to downtown Bar Harbor, where they could set up Luke's yard chairs and watch the parade from the side of the car.

"It won't be easy to get out afterward," Luke explained as they helped Wendy into the passenger side.

"That's all right," Leo affirmed. "Maybe we'll want to stick around downtown, anyway? I'm sure you've got a bar or two you could show me."

"That I do," Luke replied, his eyes shining. He looked like a little kid who'd just woken up on his birthday.

Already, downtown Bar Harbor bustled with life. Tourists and Bar Harbor residents lined the squares, dressed in red, white, and blue— often all three at once. Angie's eyes scanned the crowd, searching for her daughter, who'd said she might try to meet them downtown if she didn't feel too bad. On cue, however, a text message buzzed through.

HANNAH: I feel so pregnant today.

ANGIE: Uh oh.

ANGIE: Can I help you in any way?

HANNAH: Naw. You've got your hands full with Grandma Wendy.

HANNAH: Abby says she's working the front desk at the Keating Inn. I might go hang out with

her for a while. Put my feet up and eat the free popsicles that Nicole put in the office fridge. :P

Angie laughed, her shoulders bucking. Luke eyed her curiously.

"Oh, it's just my daughter. She's a hoot," Angie explained.

From the front seat, Leo called, "She's pretty far along by now, isn't she?"

"She's due in August," Angie explained.

"Boy or girl?"

"She doesn't want to know. As long as she or he's got ten fingers and toes, she'll be happy." Angie was particularly proud of her daughter for that.

"That's surprising in this day and age," Leo noted. "Nobody seems to have the patience for anything."

"Hannah's had to grow up quickly," Angie added, her brow furrowing. "I think that might be part of the reason."

Leo parked the car about a block from the parade route, easing into a parallel park job like a professional. It seemed appropriate that an older brother would manage something like that so well. Angie popped out of the back seat and opened the passenger side for Wendy, who blinked through the sunshine, which now seemed overly bright. Angie leafed through her purse and brought out her sunglasses, which Wendy donned. She looked like a classic older beauty, with that glistening, newly styled white hair and the large glasses. Even Leo said, "Nice look, Mom."

Luke and Leo stationed the fold-out chairs along the parade route. There was a sizzling feeling of expectation in the air. Children waved flags and jumped around or else cried into their mother's legs, overwhelmed by all the people and commotion. Angie sat next to Wendy, eyeing her, wondering if she had memories of taking Leo to such parades. Probably she did, somewhere in there.

Luke and Leo were in conversation again. Luke gestured

east, saying that a restaurant he'd previously been a part-time bartender at was just down the road.

"I'd love to take a look at it," Leo said brightly.

Luke glanced toward Angie. "The parade could come any minute."

"Oh, go on," Angie said. "You'll make it back in time."

"You'll be okay?" Luke asked doubtfully.

Angie was, frankly, hurt. "Of course! Mom and I are just fine."

Luke gave Leo a firm nod. "Okay. If we hurry, we can get back."

In a flash, the two Barrington brothers disappeared through the thick crowd. Angie twitched and dropped down to the small cooler she'd packed, drawing out two small lemonades. She passed one to Wendy, who took it but didn't make a motion to open it.

"Do you need help?" Angie asked.

Wendy shook her head slowly, her eyes becoming wider. Around them, the crowd shifted closer and closer, with people even standing in front of them. Next came the purring sound of drums in the marching band as they drew closer and closer. Trumpet players and trombonists came along, pounding through "The Stars and Stripes Forever". As Wendy's panic mounted, Angie felt the song became more sinister. She reached for her mother's lemonade and placed it on the ground, replacing it with her own hand.

"Mom? Mom?" Angie's voice broke.

Wendy's eyes filled with tears. Angie draped her body over her, holding her like a small child. Wendy quivered in her arms as the crowd surged and pulsed around them, clapping their hands in time to the marching band. God, it was loud. It was too much.

The music lasted for what seemed like forever. Throughout, tears lapped across Wendy's cheeks. Angie couldn't figure out what to do. There was no way through the thick crowd. And besides, where could they go? She didn't have the keys to Leo's car.

All she could do was hold onto her mother until the violent moment passed.

All she could do was comfort her in this moment of pain and horror.

All she could do was shove away the thoughts that, well, this was something her mother had never managed to do with her. *How frightened had Angie been at that orphanage as a toddler? How much had she wanted this very woman beside her to comfort her?*

She abandoned you, a voice told her. *Does she deserve this?*

But when Angie lifted her head to find her mother's gaze, compassion overwhelmed her. It didn't matter if Wendy "deserved this" or not. In Angie's heart, there was an immense feeling of love for this woman. *How could she refuse that?* Love was always the answer. It was always enough.

Chapter Two

"Abby. Don't be like that. Tell me the truth. Are they cankles? Do I actually have cankles?"

Hannah lay across a chaise lounge, deep enough in the shadows behind the Keating Inn front desk that made it difficult for guests to see her. Her pregnant belly was a mountain between herself and her legs. On her stomach, she propped up her book and tried to distract herself from her throbbing feet, her heartburn, and her perpetual desire to eat as Abby answered questions, checked people in, and gave instructions about how to get to the Fourth of July Parade. But her ankles, so thick and now throbbing like her feet, demanded her attention.

Abby, who'd done her darnedest to be kind and patient with Hannah all afternoon, pursed her lips. "You don't have cankles, Hannah."

"They're thicker than my thighs," Hannah pointed out.

"They are not."

Hannah groaned and dropped her head back on the chaise longue, allowing her book to tumble to the floor. *Who was she kidding?* She could hardly concentrate; comprehending two sentences in a row was a non-pregnant person's game.

"Just tell me they'll shrink back after the baby comes," Hannah groaned.

The bell over the front door jangled. Abby turned and flashed a big smile as two more guests entered.

"Welcome to the Keating Inn and Acadia Eatery! Happy Fourth of July!"

"Thank you!" The couple responded joyously, right before the woman propped up her purse on the front desk and said, "We were hoping to catch your lunch specials here at the Acadia Eatery."

"Wonderful," Abby returned. "I take it you've already been down to the parade?"

"We have. And gosh, what a show! You Bar Harbor folks really know how to celebrate," the woman affirmed cheerily. In fact, she was so sweet that Hannah thought she might vomit.

Abby laughed good-naturedly. It was difficult to tell if Abby was faking it. She had to be, right? Nobody could laugh so genuinely all day long. Even women without cankles.

Abby told the couple to head back to the Acadia Eatery, where the Fourth of July lunch specials included spareribs, New England Clam Chowder, mixed salads with gleaming pink salmon, and various types of pies slathered with whipped cream. Abby's mother, Nicole, was head chef at the Acadia Eatery, despite never having attended any sort of culinary school. In truth, Hannah really loved this about Nicole— that she'd jumped out of her old life in Portland and grabbed hold of the Keating Inn and Acadia Eatery, grateful for the opportunity to build a new life.

If Hannah had any energy at all, perhaps she'd figure out a way to do the same.

After the young couple disappeared into the Acadia Eatery,

Abby crumpled into a ball on the floor behind the front desk and dropped her head back on the flat wood.

"What's up?" Hannah let out a laugh of surprise.

"It's just exhausting, having to pretend to be happy all day long," Abby breathed, barely loud enough for Hannah to hear.

Hannah's baby popped a foot into the side of her stomach. She winced and tapped her belly back, a *hello*.

"I can't even imagine," Hannah said. "But you make it look easy."

"Well." Abby shrugged. "This is the only job I know. After I lost my job and my relationship back in Providence, I went to a dark, dark place. Moved in with Aunt Casey. Fell apart. Found myself watching five hours of HBO every single night and eating popcorn for dinner."

"Popcorn? Gosh, I'd kill for some popcorn right now."

Abby snorted with laughter, clearly grateful for the joke. Humor, Hannah knew, was often the only way through anxious feelings, a way to pick fun at yourself and remain in the present.

Hannah had only heard whispers about this era of Abby's life post-Providence, during which she and Nicole hadn't even spoken. Casey had kept news of Abby staying at her place a secret out of respect for Abby. As Hannah and her own mother, Angie, hadn't spoken for many, many months the previous year, she felt a kinship to Abby and her story. She understood what it felt like to not understand what came next.

"So, anyway," Abby finished. "I'm just grateful for this job. Even if it's not exactly what I saw myself doing in my twenties."

Hannah groaned and placed her hand at the top of her pregnant belly. "Ditto."

Abby chuckled and drew a curl around her ear. "Be right back." She disappeared through the shadows, leaving Hannah alone behind the front desk. Thirty seconds later, she returned with a caramel and chocolate ice cream on a stick, which she passed over to Hannah. Hannah shrieked with joy.

"What!"

Abby snickered. "Mom bought a package of them during that insane hot spell we had last week."

Hannah yanked off the wrapping, closed her eyes, and wrapped her lips around the top of the chocolate-coated icy delight. She was instantly transported to long-lost summer days in Chicago, back when she'd been a kid with scabbed knees, two parents who'd been in love, and her entire life ahead of her. There was no getting that back.

"Do you ever think about your ex?" Abby asked suddenly, yanking Hannah out of her reverie.

Hannah's eyes popped open. Her tongue was frozen with ice cream. As she swallowed, a flashing image of her ex came into her mind: so volatile, so angry— yet also so confident and sure of himself in a way that had captivated her, at least in the beginning.

"Ah. The father of my child? All the time."

Abby buzzed her lips. "I think about my ex all the time, too. It's pathetic. I think it's because I told myself the story of our future so many times. I'm still mourning the loss of that future. I haven't figured out a new story yet."

Hannah had never heard that feeling described so perfectly. She licked the ice cream contemplatively and added, "My feelings of loss are probably more related to music school."

"Oh yeah?"

"Yeah. I was good. Damn good. And I gave it up for, what? Partying with some absolute losers?" She shook her head, at a loss. "I wish I could shake that girl and tell her just how much she'll lose if she keeps heading down that road."

Abby shook her head. "You can't make yourself miserable

with those thoughts. Besides. Next month, you'll have your baby."

Hannah's heart stretched wider, filling the space behind her ribcage. Although, in many ways, she dreaded the end of this pregnancy and all the chaos that would ensue, her heart and mind and body already ached with love for this baby. She now understood her mother far more than she had throughout her childhood and teenage years. This was a love that transcended everything else. It was pure power.

More guests entered and demanded Abby's attention. Hannah dropped her feet to the side of the chaise longue and checked her phone for messages from her mother, who was at the parade with her own mother— a woman she so wanted to build a relationship with. To Hannah, this was a tragic wish. Wendy Barrington had dropped Angie off at the orphanage, for goodness sake. Now, dementia clouded her mind. What did Angie hope would come out of this?

Still, it's not that Hannah could blame her mother for wanting to try. Angie had lost so much over the past year— her husband, her band, and her father. Together, Angie and Hannah had decided to move halfway across the country to start over. Neither of them could have comprehended how difficult that would be.

Beneath the front desk sat a large Canon camera, something worth upward of two thousand dollars, at least. Hannah stood up, forcing herself to look away from her cankles, and walked toward the camera. It was bulky, the plastic cold in her hands. She turned it on and lifted it to snap a photo of Abby as she clacked her fingers over the front desk keyboard, checking something for another guest. Abby flashed her a dark look that said: *don't you dare.*

But when the guest left, Hannah turned the camera around to show off the preview. "You look beautiful, Abs. Like a professional woman who knows what she's doing and what she wants."

Abby inspected it, her eyebrows tight over her eyes. "You caught a pretty good angle."

Hannah laughed. "I used to take photographs as a teenager. I almost forgot about it till now."

"I took a few college photography classes," Abby said, her eyes brightening. Before Hannah could stop her, she leaped back, sitting on the front desk itself to capture a better angle of pregnant Hannah.

Hannah yelped after the flash as her eyes filled with light. "What the heck!"

"Fair's fair," Abby shot back, assessing the photo. "And besides. You haven't taken any pregnancy photos, have you?"

Hannah laughed, but it wasn't a pretty laugh— it was one of regret and sorrow. "I don't really have the money for something like that. Besides, those photos usually feature the father with his hands around the belly, right?"

Hannah imitated the familiar poses, which she'd seen all over social media.

Abby shrugged. "I'm just saying that you should have at least a few beautiful photos of yourself during this time."

"Unfortunately, I'm not one of those glowing pregnant ladies," Hannah shot back, gesturing down to her ankles. "Remember?"

Abby rolled her eyes into the back of her head. "You. Are. Glowing." She lifted the camera again and snapped another photograph of Hannah. "I mean, come on. Look at this!"

Abby turned the camera around to show the preview. Hannah didn't dare look. She stared at the far wall, wrinkling her nose.

"If I look at it, I won't be able to sleep for a week."

"I'm telling you, Hannah. Just look at it!"

Hannah groaned as she dropped her eyes back to the screen. To her surprise, however, the woman who stood just off-center in the photograph was, in fact, a "glowing pregnant woman." Her figure was like a pregnant Greek goddess in an old painting.

"You look like Mother Earth herself," Abby teased, watching Hannah's expression.

Hannah lifted her eyes back toward Abby's. Her own were damp with tears that she refused to let fall.

"Abby, you're just so talented."

"I don't know. A photographer is only as good as her subject."

"I don't think that's the saying at all," Hannah shot back. She then placed her teeth upon her lower lip, eyeing the space between herself and Abby. She no longer felt the sharp weight in her ankles. "Abby, lean up against that far wall by the bookshelf," she instructed.

Abby laughed. "Are you serious?"

"Yeah. I see a good shot there." Hannah pointed, her eyebrows lifting. "Come on!"

"All right! All right!" Abby hustled toward the bookshelf, leaning herself against the wall. "Like this?"

"A bit. Cock your head to the right?"

"Like this?"

"Yeah." Hannah lifted the camera and took several shots, framing Abby within the greater Keating Inn foyer. When she inspected the previews, her heart pounded with a once-familiar feeling.

This was what it felt like to create art. As a full-time musician, she'd previously experienced this every single day of her life.

Gosh, she'd missed it.

Abby hustled back to check out the shot. She made a soft sound in her throat.

"What does that mean?" Hannah asked. Her blood pressure spiked with anxiety.

"Oh. It's just that they're really interesting," Abby breathed. "The angles you've created and the way you've played with the sunlight in the foyer— it's very artful."

"Yeah?"

"I could imagine my photography instructor back in college using this as an example of well-constructed photography," Abby affirmed.

Hannah could hardly breathe. A small part of her prayed that Abby hadn't just said all that to make her feel better about her cankles.

Over the next half-hour, Abby and Hannah flung themselves into a state of perpetual artmaking. They photographed one another in various spaces across the foyer, hallway, and entryway of the Acadia Eatery— playing with light and angles and fine-tuning what Abby remembered from her photography classes. Hannah hadn't had such fun in months.

"Hello? Is anyone here?" A voice rang out from the foyer as Abby finished a photograph in the hallway between the Eatery and the Inn.

"Oh shoot. I'm neglecting my real job," Abby muttered with a laugh. She turned and headed back for the front desk as Hannah waddled behind her, her heart brimming with happiness.

When Hannah rounded the corner, she found Abby in conversation with a younger couple in their mid-twenties. The couple was clearly from money. You could see it in the shine of the woman's dark hair and the cut and style of the man's shoes. Hannah was accustomed to seeing people with money at the Keating Inn. It was always disconcerting for her, a woman who had so little of it.

Abby was in the midst of apologizing for having abandoned her station.

"Oh, honey. It's no trouble!" The woman showed very bright teeth. "Were you taking photographs for the inn?"

Abby brightened. "Yes. We need new photographs for the website and our social media." She then gestured toward Hannah and added, "Hannah has a gorgeous photographer's eye. She captures the light better than Vincent Van Gogh."

The woman cocked her head, interested. Rich people always loved Vincent Van Gogh. Hannah knew this was ironic since Van Gogh had died absolutely penniless.

"So, you run a photography business alongside your work here at the Keating Inn?" the woman asked.

Hannah suddenly blurted, "Yes. We do." She put on her cheeriest smile, pretending to be one of those women who just smiled for no reason at all.

The woman gave her boyfriend a bug-eyed look. The man hardly seemed to understand her expression.

"Honey. Are you thinking what I'm thinking?" the woman asked him.

"I think so," the man returned; although Hannah would have bet twenty bucks, he had no idea.

The woman returned her gaze to Abby and Hannah. "We're newly engaged."

"Congratulations!" Abby said brightly.

"Thank you," the woman returned, beaming. The man remained stony-faced. "The thing is, we want something really special for our engagement photos. We live in Brooklyn, and all of our friends have really traditional engagement shots across Brooklyn. Like, ugh, if I see another engagement photo in front of the Brooklyn Bridge, I'll scream!"

"Totally." Abby nodded.

"See? I figured you'd understand that," the woman said. "When we arrived in Bar Harbor this morning, I was like, this is it. This is the place for our photos. I had plans to research local photographers later this afternoon, but if the two of you are up for it..."

"Oh, of course," Hannah replied before she was even aware she had anything to say.

"Yes," Abby affirmed, casting Hannah a confused yet grateful smile. "We have a very special package for engaged couples."

The woman grimaced. Hurriedly, Hannah added, "But the thing is, we never duplicate the locations. It just makes it more special and not redundant."

"Right," Abby added. "We know you want a personalized experience."

"Yes." The woman nodded quickly, making her hair wave around every which way.

"We know all the best locations," Hannah added, boosting their non-existent brand.

"I had a wonderful feeling when I saw the two of you," the woman continued. "Like you two would just instinctively get it." She reached into her purse and removed a Chanel wallet. She then removed a card, which she placed delicately in Abby's hand. "This is my business card. Shoot me a message, and we can set up a time to meet later this week and discuss your rates. We'll be here at the Keating Inn until Saturday."

The woman then turned to her fiancé and lifted her fist with triumph. "No more Brooklyn Bridge photos, baby!"

The man tried to smile back, but the corners of his lips didn't quite make it.

The woman reached out to splay a hand across Abby's shoulder. "It was fate that we met today. I truly believe that."

Abby held the card, trying and failing to make her face calm down. The woman continued to blink at her with a big smile. Hannah wanted to joke that she looked possessed.

Finally, the woman said, "But could you actually check us in?"

Abby laughed, tossing her head back. "Gosh, of course! I forgot about my other job for a moment. Let's head to the front desk, shall we?"

Hannah watched as the engaged couple and Abby headed back toward Abby's post at the mahogany front desk. From a distance, Hannah watched them, her heart swelling with promise. She wasn't entirely sure if her baby could understand her thoughts or not, but she often sent them down there anyway.

Maybe this is a fresh start, baby. Maybe we'll be all right, after all.

Chapter Three

"Here. Drink this." Angie passed her mother an ice-cold glass of water and watched as the old woman's eyes closed, her throat clenching and unclenching as she drank. They stood in the shadows of the Keating House nearly an hour after Wendy's panic attack during the parade. Exhaustion had drained both of them. For her part, Angie prayed that Wendy couldn't remember the terrifying time she'd had.

Luke's footsteps made the floorboards creak. He entered the kitchen from the foyer, Heather's keys jangling.

"We're the only ones here," he explained to Leo and Angie. "Heather's off to visit her daughters, Nicole's up at the Eatery, and Casey's in Spain for an architecture project."

Leo scrubbed his hand through his fraying hair and eyed their mother. Luke assessed him, opened the fridge, and removed two beers. As he passed one to Leo, Leo grunted his thanks.

"I figured you needed one just as much as I did," Luke explained.

Perhaps the parade idea had been a disaster. Angie draped her hand over her mother's shoulder and helped her toward the living room, where she collapsed on the couch nearest the bay window, her eyes toward the black television.

"Luke? Do you mind if we turn this on?" Angie called.

Luke hurried to find the remote. Leo joined them, leaning against the doorway between the kitchen and the living room. "She likes daytime television. Soap operas. Anything like that. It usually calms her down when something like this happens."

Luke nodded, clicking the remote and turning the channel as quickly as possible. When he reached a soap opera, Wendy leaned forward, the skin around her eyes crinkling.

"She likes this one," Leo affirmed. "In case you can't tell."

"Leave it on," Wendy requested daintily. "Please." She then looked at Luke as though he was a stranger, giving him a nod of approval. Luke's eyes grew damp as he placed the remote on the little table beside her, next to Heather's piles of books.

Back in the kitchen, the three Barrington siblings listened to the television's over-dramatic soap opera music. Angie poured herself a glass of wine and joined her brothers, eyeing the table between their beverages and cursing the optimism she'd had for the day. She knew better than that. The only way to have a good day was to expect nothing.

"She seems calmer, now," Angie tried, although she immediately regretted it.

Leo sniffed and sipped his beer. Angie stared out the window, imagining the chaos downtown. Within the next few hours, there would be a hot dog eating contest, a costume contest, a pie contest, a short sailing race, and, last but not least, a fireworks display. An image of her and her mother eating a slice of blueberry pie at that contest— something Angie had made up in that optimistic brain of hers— died.

"Whose house is this again?" Leo asked. His words were somewhere between a cough and a grunt.

"My girlfriend and her sisters live here," Luke explained. "The property was left to them after their Uncle Joseph passed away last year."

Leo sniffed.

"Joseph and Adam Keating used to own a lot of properties across Bar Harbor," Luke continued nervously. "But Adam got involved with a woman who managed to take so much of what was his. She sold much of it to the Snow family and then squandered that money."

Angie piped up. "That woman was Heather's real mother?"

Luke nodded. "Although she's stopped thinking about it that way. She was raised by Adam's first wife, a woman named Jamie."

"Complicated," Leo said softly, as though their situation wasn't complicated in the least.

"We know all about that," Angie reminded him.

There was silence. Angie immediately regretted having brought up their strange family dynamic.

Suddenly, in the next room, there came the sound of a twinkling piano. Angie's heart surged. The first few notes seemed tentative, but soon after, the fingers behind the notes took on greater strength. Angie jumped from the kitchen table and hustled in to find Wendy seated at the piano, her head bent and her eyes closed. It was as though the music flowed through her without fully asking permission from her sick mind.

When Angie had first discovered the musicianship of her mother, her heart had cracked into a million little pieces. Throughout the many years of her music career, her adoptive father had belittled it, saying it was a "nothing" career. All the while, her talents had been genetic, passed down from a mother who hadn't wanted her.

It was a complicated feeling.

Angie stepped up beside her mother on the bench, watching her fingers as they scuttled over the keys, playing Mozart. Angie's heart seized. She glanced back toward Leo and asked, "What kind of studies have they done about dementia patients and music?"

To this, Leo only shrugged. "She still finds it in her to play. It's miraculous. But the doctors don't know how much longer it will last."

Angie's eyes dampened. After a dramatic pause, she dropped down beside Wendy and placed her fingers on the lower notes, harmonizing along with her mother. Just like any other professional musician, her mother took the cue and began to work with Angie's chords, creating something that was part Mozart, part-Angie and Wendy. Angie's heart beat in time to the music as her eyes closed.

Was this really happening? How could this be?

They played for a good five minutes. Angie could have continued like that for an hour, maybe two. What a magical thing it was to be able to "jam" with your mother. Angie often felt that jamming transcended conversation or rational thought. It was the ultimate form of creativity.

When Wendy spontaneously stopped playing, Angie begged herself not to cry. She splayed her hands across her lap and eyed her mother curiously, wondering if Wendy would say something about the jam session. Instead, Wendy turned her eyes back to the television, which Luke or Leo had turned off while mother and daughter had played. She scowled and pointed.

"Where did my soap go?"

Angie's heart cracked. Leo hustled for the remote to turn the television back on. Slowly, Wendy stood to her feet and hobbled back to the couch, her eyes on the television screen. It was almost as though nothing had happened.

Angie crept back toward the kitchen, watching her mother take another drink of water. When she reached the doorway, she nearly stumbled into Leo.

Leo seemed to sense what was on her mind.

"Don't beat yourself up about it," he ordered, sounding stern.

Angie wanted to ask him: *how?* But she supposed that was a stupid question. She returned to the kitchen table and drank half of her glass of wine. Her soul felt as though it lingered somewhere in the back of her skull, exhausted from the events of the day.

Luke and Leo joined her. Luke said something about having "missed out on" the musical talents of their genes. Leo joked he had, as well. Angie sipped more wine and refilled her glass, wondering if it was rude to just go upstairs and crash in one of Heather, Casey, Nicole, or Abby's beds.

Suddenly, Leo hit them with a bomb.

"Part of the reason I came here today is that I think we're getting to the end," Leo said these words easily, as though they meant nothing at all.

But Angie and Luke gaped at him, both shocked.

Leo sipped his beer. "She hardly knows where she is anymore. There are hours of clarity and then hours and hours of nothingness. It's getting difficult to deal with."

Angie's face spontaneously scrunched into a ball. Her inner voice begged her not to cry. *But how could she stop it?* She hardly knew how to love this woman properly; now, she was about to die.

"What do you plan to do?" Luke asked.

"I want to put her in a home with a memory clinic," Leo informed them. "There are a number of options around Boston."

Luke nodded. Angie wanted to punch his arm, although she wasn't sure why. *Did she really expect Leo to understand how to handle someone with dementia? Did she really expect either herself or Luke to make up the difference?*

"That makes sense," Luke replied, then rubbed the back of his neck.

But Angie heard herself reason, "There are a number of memory clinics here in Bar Harbor, as well."

Both Luke and Leo gazed at her as though she had three heads. Angie swallowed another bit of wine and reasoned with both them and herself.

"Leo, you've taken such good care of our mother over the years," she began, scarcely able to believe herself as she spoke. "Luke and I only just learned of her existence earlier this year."

"That couldn't be helped," Leo told her, his face growing shadowed.

"I know that. I know that." She waved a hand. "No one is to blame for everything that's happened."

Well, assuredly, there was someone to blame. Probably, that blame fell on their deceased father's shoulders. But that was a whole other story, wasn't it?

"If you bring her to Bar Harbor, Luke and I will pick up the slack on caring for her and visiting her," Angie continued. "You can come up here to visit both her and us whenever you like. You can even stay for weeks at a time if you want to." She glanced at Luke, who had begun to nod, catching on. "I know Luke and I would like to get to know our brother better. This would give us a chance to do that."

Leo's eyes were stormy. He sucked down the rest of his beer and tapped his knuckle on the table.

"How long does she have?" Luke murmured.

Angie braced herself. This wasn't news she wanted to hear.

"The doctor said six months to a year," Leo breathed.

Angie's heart seized. She dropped her eyes to the table,

terrified, yet again, of losing a parent. She'd already gone through that chaos twice.

Funeral planning. Music selection. Greeting people she'd never known, all who said, "I'm so terribly sorry for your loss."

God, could she take it?

"How much a month are the Boston memory clinics?" Luke asked.

"About six thousand," Leo told him. "As far as I can tell, that's pretty standard across the United States."

"Six thousand dollars per month." Angie held the words across her tongue. "Incredible."

"It's exorbitant," Luke shot out. "During a family's darkest times, they're supposed to come up with six thousand extra dollars per month?"

"It's evil," Leo affirmed.

The three Barrington siblings held the thought for a long time as the silence grew heavy around them. In the other room, Wendy continued to watch her television soap opera, perhaps the only thing that kept her rooted in any kind of reality.

"But I know that we can do it," Angie said suddenly, her stomach seizing.

In truth: *how could they possibly manage that?* She and Hannah worked odd jobs at the Keating Inn; Angie often played the piano for cash at The Minty Green, a jazz club in Portland; they also picked up odd shifts across town and pitched all the money together that they could. Even still, they lived in one of the dankest apartments in Bar Harbor, with a rent of eight hundred and fifty dollars in total, an amount they could hardly gather together.

"Agreed," Luke said.

Angie's nostrils flared. She and Luke looked at Leo, both breathless.

"So that means about two thousand per month," Leo said tentatively. "For each of us."

"Exactly," Luke said.

"Here in Bar Harbor?" Leo continued, incredulous.

"Here in Bar Harbor," Angie affirmed.

Leo dropped his eyes to the table, studying the tips of his fingers. Angie and Luke locked eyes, both incredulous. *Had they really just convinced Leo to do this?* Had they really just agreed to a bill of two thousand dollars per month for the final care of their very sick, yet very "new" mother?

"I can't think of a reason not to agree to this," Leo breathed finally, locking his eyes with Angie's. "I know she can feel the love you two have for her. And now that I've retired, there's no reason that I can't spend much more time up here."

Angie drew her hand over his, squeezing it softly as her eyes filled with tears.

"Just let me figure some stuff out for us in Boston," Leo said finally, flicking a tear from his cheek. "Maybe we can make it work sometime in August."

"August suits us just fine," Luke replied.

Angie's stomach twisted, realizing the weight that August 2022 would bring. Not only would Hannah give birth, but her mother would also move to Bar Harbor for good.

It was difficult to imagine how they would possibly make this work.

But when she locked eyes with Luke a final time, he gave her a firm nod. There was no question about it. They were a family, and they would find a way through this pain. Somehow.

Chapter Four

The card the young woman had given Abby and Hannah read:

Candace Waterloo
    Interior Designer
    4767 71st Ave.
    New York, New York
    candacewaterloo@cwl.ny

"New York money," Abby affirmed a couple of days after the Fourth, slipping the card onto Hannah's kitchen table. Hannah had convinced herself to get over the shame of her dank apartment and invite Abby over.

"Manhattan money," Hannah repeated, watching as Abby typed out an email to Candace, sending along several edited photographs that the two had taken to make sure that Candace approved of their artistic style before officially hiring them. They'd even gone above and beyond, taking photographs of surrounding areas in Bar Harbor, including several "top secret" locations that they promised would belong to Candace and her fiancé alone.

In short: it was more work than Hannah had done since her stomach had ballooned into full-on pregnant mode. But because Abby was such a diligent worker (and Hannah needed the money terribly), she fought through the weight, forcing her thick ankles forward and taking photograph after photograph.

"Oh my God. She already wrote back!" Abby cried a few minutes later.

"What are you girls doing in here?" Angie appeared from her bedroom, wearing only a massive white t-shirt and a pair of slippers. She retrieved a cardboard container of orange juice and grabbed a glass, eyeing Abby and Hannah curiously.

"Come on! What did she say?" Hannah demanded, ignoring her mother.

Abby's cheeks reddened with excitement. "She says she 'totally adores them' and thinks we have 'a really interesting eye'!" She used her fingers to form quotations and even mocked the woman's New York City accent. Hannah had to admit that she sounded just like her.

"You're kidding!" Hannah wanted to jump up from her chair but held herself back, brimming with happiness. Her baby pumped its foot against her belly, sharing in on the joy.

"I'm not." Abby smashed her fist against her thigh and winced. "Oh gosh. I'm overwhelmed."

Angie poured the three of them glasses of juice and positioned them out across the table. "Are you going to tell me what's going on? Or leave me in the dark?"

Abby sipped her juice, dying her top lip neon orange. "We were screwing around the other day."

"As we do," Hannah teased.

"Taking photographs and stuff. I had no idea that Hannah was so skilled with a camera."

"Oh, yes." Angie shook her head furiously. "She was always taking photos of her dad and I. If she hadn't gone into music..." She trailed off, glancing at Hannah, who couldn't bring herself to look at her mother.

Gosh, she'd disappointed her mother.

"Anyway. This young couple entered and asked if we take photographs," Abby continued, forcing herself through the awkward pause. "Professionally."

"And you said yes?" Angie asked, aghast.

"Don't worry," Abby returned quickly. "We sent along photos to make sure she likes our work."

"And she... hired you?" Angie asked, her eyes buggy.

"She just asked what our rate is," Abby said, furrowing her brow. Her gaze locked with Hannah's. "I wish I knew what to ask for."

Hannah glanced at her mother, standing there so vulnerable with her naked legs beneath her white t-shirt, no makeup, her own lips now stained with juice. Angie had just confessed that she needed to drum up upward of two thousand dollars per month for her mother's medical bills, starting in August or September. With Hannah's baby on the way, the money pressure was more intense than ever.

"We have to ask for real money," Hannah said under her breath. "New York money. Like you said."

Abby's cheeks were now tomato-red. She locked eyes with Angie for some kind of sign.

"The music photographers we usually worked with in Chicago gave us a deal," Angie said with a shrug. "They knew we weren't exactly on the high end of the pay scale."

"But these people are," Abby breathed.

"A thousand," Hannah said firmly, her fist on the table.

Angie's jaw dropped. "Really?"

"I think it's too low, honestly," Hannah shot back, her confidence growing.

Angie and Abby exchanged glances. Obviously, neither of them had made one thousand dollars per day, ever.

"What if we make it sound a little bit different," Abby suggested conspiratorially, her fingers on the keyboard.

"I'm all ears," Hannah said.

"Four hundred dollars an hour," Abby started to explain. "Our first package is two hours. Our second is between three and four."

"So they can choose for themselves..." Angie whispered. "I love it."

"Me too," Hannah added, her thoughts purring with excitement. "Write that down. Now."

Angie snapped her fingers. "You girls need a website."

"And an official name," Abby cried.

"God, a name is hard," Angie breathed. "It's just like choosing a band name. Do you know how long it took us to come up with ours back in Chicago? I swear that was half the pain of getting kicked out of the band. I'd come up with that name. Now, it doesn't belong to me anymore."

Hannah's stomach stirred with sorrow. Although she wanted to support her mother in every conceivable way, it wasn't exactly comfortable to hear her discuss the horrors of her divorce from Hannah's father. According to Angie, Hannah's father had broken things off with the woman he'd been having an affair with— the bass player in their band. Hannah wanted nothing to do with him. She often wondered if that was the "right way" or if forgiveness was the better plan.

But right now, with her father halfway across the country, a baby on the way, and a new career blossoming out from under her, she figured her father didn't matter.

Within the hour, Candace wrote back.

Abby and Hannah,

Godfrey and I would like a large selection of photographs. The three-to-four-hour package sounds perfect.

Shall we meet in the foyer of the Keating Inn tomorrow afternoon after lunch? Around two?

Abby and Hannah locked eyes and shrieked. Their voices bounced around the closet-sized kitchen of their downtown apartment, which played out such a contrast to the enormous Keating House, where Abby lived out her days with her mother and aunts.

"This is insane," Abby muttered, writing back to confirm the time. "Absolutely insane."

* * *

It truly was.

The following day at noon, Hannah donned a black swing dress and a pair of black tennis shoes and waited outside her apartment building for Abby to pick her up. Out beyond Bar Harbor, Frenchman Bay glittered joyously beneath the July sunlight, beckoning Hannah and her sore ankles into its gorgeous depths.

But she had work to do.

Abby tapped the horn of her mother's car. The beep-beep pinged around Main Street so that every tourist and passer-by lifted their eyes to see the pregnant Hannah waving her hand exuberantly as Abby stopped the car in front of the apartment block. As Hannah slipped in, Abby bobbed her head in time to the music and pumped her fist.

"This is the first day of the rest of our lives, baby!" Abby cried.

Hannah, ever a smart aleck, returned with, "Why are you talking to my baby? I'm right here!"

Abby rolled her eyes and pressed the gas, whipping them back to the Keating Inn and Acadia Eatery. Hannah dropped her head against the car seat headrest as the wind from Frenchman Bay cut through the partly opened window and fluttered her hair.

"I saw Candace this morning," Abby explained on the way. "She told me she bought five new outfits yesterday, just for the shoot."

Hannah snorted. "I can't remember the last time I bought a single outfit, let alone five."

"She might be difficult to work with," Abby said with a shrug. "We have to keep an open mind and remember that she's paying us a whole lot more than we're used to." She cast Hannah a dark and knowing look.

"I know, I know." Hannah waved her hands. "I'll behave myself. I'm not always so..."

"Articulate about your feelings?" Abby said with a funny laugh.

"Abby. The entire time you've known me, I've been pregnant," Hannah pointed out. "You have to cut me some slack."

"All right. Slack, officially cut." Abby gave Hannah a crooked smile.

Back at the Keating Inn and Acadia Eatery, Casey, who'd recently returned from her trip to Spain, greeted them from the front desk. Her mouth stretched wide into a yawn as she explained that she was "super jet-lagged but glad to be back." Abby fell into a hug and explained what she and Hannah were up to that afternoon as Hannah shifted around awkwardly behind her. She knew her mother was officially Luke's sister and that Luke was sort of a part of the Harvey-Keating Clan. But that didn't always make Hannah feel officially welcomed.

This, according to Angie, would just take time to fix and was more Hannah and Angie's fault than anyone else's. "We're just a bit shyer than the Harvey Sisters," Angie had said once to Hannah. "Just a bit more closed off. We'll have to try to fix that."

Nicole appeared in the hallway between the Keating Inn and Acadia Eatery and beckoned for Abby and Hannah to approach. "I just made you two some extra-bougie grilled cheese sandwiches," Nicole said conspiratorially, placing her arms on both Abby and Hannah's shoulders as they walked. "Brie, cheddar, and goat cheese, with caramelized onions and spinach," she explained. "Plus, salt and vinegar chips."

"My mouth is watering," Hannah moaned.

Nicole laughed, her eyes dancing. "I just figured you'd need your strength for the hours ahead. I've had a couple of conversations with this Candace Waterloo. She's a handful. She made me change half the menu just for her and her fiancé."

Abby wrinkled her nose and cast Hannah a worried look. "We'll be able to handle her. Won't we?"

It was difficult to say.

In the wake of the gorgeous sandwiches and salt and vinegar chips, Hannah and Abby waited for the young couple nervously. They'd decided to bring two cameras— both Canons, both belonging to the Keating Inn and Acadia Eatery. "It makes us look more professional if we both have a camera," Abby had insisted. Hannah had agreed. "We can get multiple angles at once."

"Where are we driving first again?" Hannah asked, suddenly terrified that she'd forgotten their itinerary, which they'd perfectly constructed the evening before.

"We're driving all the way to the secret beach first," Abby affirmed. "Little Hunters Beach."

"They're going to love it," Hannah affirmed. "When you first took me there, I freaked."

"You asked if we'd died and gone to heaven." Abby chortled.

"Living in Bar Harbor is very unreal sometimes," Hannah pointed out.

"It's true."

"There they are!" Candace appeared at the bottom of the vintage circular staircase with her thin arms pointed toward the sky. Behind her, her fiancé carried not one, but two suitcases, his shoulders hunched with the weight. He wore a simple yet chic black suit jacket and a white V-neck shirt beneath, along with a pair of jeans that looked both expensive and also, basically, just like every other pair of jeans in the world. Hannah would never understand the ultra-rich.

"You look fantastic," Abby said as the pair approached.

"Thanks." Candace flipped her hair. "I bought another outfit right before meeting you. It's just so difficult to decide. Right, honey?" She cast her fiancé, Godfrey, a funny smile.

Godfrey nodded like a puppy, eager to do whatever she pleased. Abby and Hannah were careful not to look at one another at that moment. They might have burst into laughter and ultimately destroyed their brand-new business.

They had to work diligently. They had to be on top of their game.

Abby explained their strategy as they approached Nicole's vehicle, which they planned to use for the next several hours ahead. "We have ten locations planned," she began.

"Ten?" Candace almost screeched, glancing back at her fiancé. "God, that's awesome. People in Brooklyn normally get what? Six?"

Godfrey shrugged and fell into the back of Nicole's car, buckling himself in and crossing his arms. Candace followed after him, jabbering more about the horrific state of "normal" engagement photos. Hannah listened intently, wanting to take note for any future projects. They couldn't make any mistakes.

When they reached the Little Hunters Beach, Abby and Hannah had to wait a full five minutes as Candace did a full-on freak-out about the beauty of the place, pounding Godfrey's chest with both fists as she exclaimed just how jealous everyone in Brooklyn would be. After that, she had to fix her makeup, change her clothes yet again, and demand Godfrey to stand up from his rest on a nearby rock.

Only then could Abby and Hannah begin photographing.

Once they began, they found themselves in a real groove. Hannah, being terribly pregnant, maintained a single position for most of the shoot at the secret beach, while Abby bobbed around, taking more creative shots from various angles. Throughout, Candace managed to maintain a beautiful, if stone-like smile, while Godfrey's own grin looked painful.

Even still, as Hannah flipped through the previews on the camera she'd used, her heart dropped into her stomach.

In a word, they were stunning— and that was even before the proper editing session that she and Abby had planned for that evening.

* * *

On and on the afternoon went, dipping from three hours to four. When they finally dropped the couple off at the Keating Inn and Acadia Eatery at six-fifteen, both were droopy-eyed and squabbling quietly in the back seat. Hannah listened as hard as she could to their argument and soon learned that Candace didn't think Godfrey had picked out enough outfits for their photography session. To this, Godfrey just shrugged and said, "You're the only one they'll look at, anyway." Hannah had to admit that this was a pretty good response, especially for someone as vain as Candace.

Abby parked the car outside the Keating House, turned off the engine, and then hustled around the side to help Hannah out. Hannah was grateful to grip Abby's arm and step out onto the gravel, eyeing the warm orange lights of the dining room and kitchen. She thought of her mother, far away in Portland that night, performing for The Minty Green jazz bar for a middling two hundred and fifty dollars. Together, Angie and Hannah were doing what they had to do to survive.

Back inside, Abby poured them both glasses of water and situated them on the living room couch, where Hannah dropped back on two pillows, her face pointed toward Abby's computer screen. Abby uploaded the photographs as they picked fun at the silly couple, making bets on how long their marriage would last.

"She just wants to have the dress and the party and the photographs," Hannah quipped.

"It's so typical, isn't it? I feel like a lot of girls I graduated with went through that. Plucked up whatever guy they could find in pursuit of that elusive engagement ring," Abby said.

Nicole stepped out of the kitchen with a bowl of salted popcorn. "I couldn't help but overhear!"

Hannah and Abby turned, laughing at Nicole's surprise entrance.

"And what do you think?" Hannah asked, propping her chin up on her fist.

Nicole chewed her popcorn contemplatively as she placed the bowl in front of the girls. "After what I went through, all I can say is this. Nobody should rush into marriage. It has to be a partnership, a balanced agreement. If there's any showiness about it, it might not work." Nicole lifted her shoulder into a shrug. "But who knows? The wedding is just the first step. Maybe your client will figure out a way to build happiness along the way."

Hannah and Abby cast one another doubtful glances. Nicole then bent down to check out the photographs on Abby's computer— Candace and Godfrey on top of a mountain; Candace and Godfrey with their feet in the frothing water; Candace bent over so that Godfrey could kiss her joyously in front of a gorgeous beach.

Nicole gasped with each image. "Girls! These are incredible. Who took which?"

Abby and Hannah explained their process: that Hannah had played with the light, and Abby had toyed with the angles. This had created a very interesting palate of different photographs, many of which looked fully professional.

Nicole stood to full height with her arms crossed over her chest. There was a strange silence.

"Mom. Why are you being so quiet?" Abby demanded, sounding on edge.

Nicole shook her head, her eyes glistening. "Sorry. I just had no idea what kind of talent you girls had up your sleeves." She rubbed her temple, stirring with thought. "We genuinely need help with the Keating Inn website and social media."

Abby and Hannah locked eyes, remembering what they'd told Candace already about their previous job— updating the website and social media of the Keating Inn. It was almost as though they'd created this job out of thin air.

"Are you suggesting that you want to hire us?" Abby asked with a sneaky smile.

Nicole tied her hair into a sloppy ponytail. "I guess something like this would be freelance. I can draw up a contract tomorrow."

Hannah's jaw dropped. She and Abby seemed to have a silent conversation in mid-air. Abby turned quickly to ask an additional question.

"How much can you afford to pay us? It's a family business; I get that. We don't want to overshoot what we ask for."

Hannah nodded, recognizing the conundrum. Nicole's face was stoic, her eyes searching the corners of the room as though they could tell her the correct number.

"Whatever the median rate is, add fifteen dollars an hour," Nicole said with finality.

Abby's eyes widened. She and Hannah shared a moment of

silence. Hannah's heartbeat pounded in both ears, ricocheting back and forth.

"But how many hours a week?" Hannah suddenly remembered to ask. The back of her mind screamed: *I need this. God, I need this.*

Nicole grabbed her phone and typed herself a note, her brow furrowed. When she lifted her head, she added, "I took an online course recently that explained the importance of social media these days. With everything I need to do at the Acadia Eatery, I simply don't have time to devote to it." There was a beat of silence before she added, "I think we can afford to pay you each about ten hours per week, forty-five dollars an hour, for now. Perhaps the two of you could create monthly reports to show social media engagements, clicks, and comments. After that, we can assess if the social media presence actually helps in bookings and sales."

Hannah's understanding of social media lived and died within her own social media sphere. Still, she was a twenty-first-century woman with a can-do attitude. There wasn't anything she couldn't research and figure out online.

"That won't be a problem," Hannah chirped. "And forty-five dollars an hour, ten hours per week, is a damn good place to start."

Chapter Five

Angie's set list fluttered at the top of the baby grand piano at the Portland-based jazz bar, The Minty Green. On it, she'd scribed her familiar favorites:

"Ain't Misbehavin'" by Fats Waller

"Georgia On My Mind"

"A Foggy Day (In London Town)"

"My Funny Valentine"

"Tangerine"

"There Is No Greater Love"

Over the past twenty-plus years of her career, she'd memorized these jazz standards, whipping them out for little dinner parties and intimate jazz settings. She could have played them in her sleep. As her fingers fluttered over the keys, her eyes roamed the shadowed bar, watching the couples who whispered over their cocktails, their hands locked together beneath the table. Behind the bar, the bartender watched her, nodding as he circled a white cloth around the inside of a pint glass.

This was Angie's twentieth performance at The Minty Green, a gig she'd picked up after a particularly strange incident last spring. The Harvey Sisters' cousin, Brittany, had been involved in a messy divorce from a particularly cruel man (oh, but weren't they all cruel? Angie often wondered). In the wake of Brittany kicking him out, her highly successful Bar Harbor Antiques shop was robbed of thousands and thousands of dollars of inventory. Although it was suspected that Brittany's ex was to blame, Brittany and the Harvey Sisters had needed proof.

That had come with a James Bond-esque plan: Angie, with a wire, sent into The Minty Green, where it was said that Brittany's ex often hung out.

She'd gotten the information, all right. And on top of all that mess, she'd also nabbed herself a consistent gig, one that earned her two-hundred and fifty dollars for a four-hour slot. It didn't pay many of the bills, but it wasn't terrible, either.

Two-hundred and fifty dollars per gig. In order for Angie to pay even one month of her portion of her mother's bill, she needed to rack up eight gigs. Eight. Recently, she'd played between six and seven times per month. There was a chance she could ask the bartender for additional slots. That said, she also didn't want to "rob" gigs from the other musicians on the docket, especially as there was no way of knowing what sorts of hardships they were going through, as well.

Angie played through "A Foggy Day (In London Town)" and then drifted into "My Funny Valentine," swaying with the music, draping her shoulders forward and back. According to a text she'd received that afternoon, Leo and Wendy had already arrived safely back to Boston and had begun to go through Wendy's things in preparation for her big move up the east coast. This, alone, felt like a pressing weight. Time rushed forward.

When Angie opened her eyes a bit wider, she caught sight of an unfamiliar figure toward the back of the bar. It wasn't entirely a rare thing for men or women to sit alone during jazz nights. Angie understood them the most: the contemplative bunch who wanted to wash away their sorrows and sip cocktails without the necessity of conversation. There was something a bit different about this man, however. Certainly, he was handsome, with a sparkle to his eye even from this great distance, one that made Angie stumble slightly on the keys (something she rarely ever did).

The real difference between this man and the other lonely people sitting at the bar was that he seemed rapt with attention to Angie and Angie alone. It was both chilling and thrilling at the same time. Angie forced her gaze back to the keys and demanded her own attention. *So what. The guy liked to stare.* But every time her gaze drifted back in his direction, she found him still captivated, as though Angie, herself, was the most interesting woman on the planet.

In truth, she'd never felt interesting in the slightest. The idea thrilled her.

Angie finished her set at eleven-thirty that night. It was a weekday, which meant the bar closed at twelve. She grabbed her set list and headed for the counter to order her complimentary drink, which she planned to sip slowly before heading to the attached bedroom. Since she'd taken a late-night gig three hours from Bar Harbor and was the only consistent out-of-towner who performed, it was up to her to bring her own bed sheets and provide her own toiletries. Still, the space was clean and pleasant with a pretty view of the park directly behind the little bar. It was far better than making the drive back to Bar Harbor so late at night.

"Manhattan?" the bartender asked with a clack of his knuckles on the bar top.

"Yes, sir." She smiled sleepily.

As the ice cracked into the glass, the bartender said, just as he always did, "You sounded great tonight, Ang. The crowd loved it."

Angie blushed timidly, just as she always did. "I'm just grateful for the gig." *Could she demand another set per month? Another three, perhaps?* He placed the cocktail before her and she sipped, her eyelids drooping.

A figure appeared on the barstool beside her. Angie kept her eyes on her Manhattan, building walls between herself and the crowd around her. Smalltalk had always been other people's game, not hers. The man spoke to the bartender, delivering a joke and a drink order. The bartender greeted him by the name— Fletcher, which struck Angie as particularly odd. She hadn't heard that name outside of movies, not ever.

Curiosity overwhelmed her as she glanced to her right to find the handsome stranger who'd been sitting alone, watching her. He even watched her now, wearing a sneaky smile. The bartender poured him a whiskey on the rocks, a drink that Angie respected.

Fletcher lifted it. "Wonderful set tonight."

Angie's cheeks warmed. "Thank you." She dared herself to hold his gaze. It was alarmingly delightful to look into the depths of his black eyes, which seemed like blackholes, drawing her into impossible darkness.

Fletcher gestured toward the stool beside her. "Do you mind if I sit for a moment?"

"The bar will be closed soon," Angie told him timidly, giving him an out.

"Yes, I'm aware, but that doesn't matter." Fletcher took this as an invitation, dropping onto the stool with that grin still plastered across his face.

Angie turned her eyes back to her cocktail, suddenly overwhelmed and unable to keep her own dare. *What did this man want with her?*

"I take it this isn't your first rodeo," Fletcher began, his words bouncing flirtatiously.

"No." Angie couldn't look at him. "I've been playing piano since I was a little girl."

"I imagine you don't always play alone."

The words were taut with expectation. Angie tilted her head. "No. I hardly did over the years."

Why had she told him that?

He nodded. "Don't get me wrong. The act works well. A beautiful woman, alone at the piano, playing sad jazz love songs. That said, in a place like this, it's just background music for bad dates."

Angie arched her brow and turned to face him once more. Back and forth. It already felt like a strange game.

"I don't think that's entirely true," Angie countered.

For a split second, Fletcher's smile faltered. His smile shimmered with confusion.

"That is, I don't think they're all on bad dates," Angie tried to joke, gesturing out across the shadowed floor.

Fletcher tossed his head back excitedly, the flat of his stomach jumping with laughter. He spoke off to the side to the bartender as he counted through the bills of the register. "She's funny."

The bartender, busy with his calculation, didn't respond.

"Tell me, Angie," Fletcher began, using her name for the first time. (She had introduced herself immediately before her performance.)

Angie's heart pounded with intrigue as she watched him lift his whiskey, tilting the glass around and around. He held the silence for no more than five seconds, but the weight of each moment seemed horrifically heavy. She couldn't take it.

"Tell me how you ended up playing all alone?"

Angie hadn't expected that sort of question. The answer to it was the tip of the iceberg of the rest of her messy little life. She sipped her Manhattan and considered this, listening to the soft twinkling of the music the bartender had put over the stereo. Compared to live music, it sounded sterile.

"I left behind my old life, my old marriage, and my old band," Angie finally told him, choosing honesty over everything else. "It's left me alone. Just me, my piano, and my jazz standards."

Fletcher whistled, impressed. "That's a whole lot to lose at once."

Angie wanted to say: *you're telling me.* But she remained silent, not wanting to sound stupid or silly.

Instead, all of a sudden, an old poem she'd always loved by Elizabeth Bishop popped into her head. "The art of losing isn't hard to master. So many things are filled with the intent to be lost, that their loss is no disaster."

The sparkle behind Fletcher's eyes ignited. His smile, probably false, filtered out. He looked at her as though she was the only woman in the world.

"That is so well said."

Angie shrugged. "Elizabeth Bishop is the best."

Fletcher shook his head. "But you're the one who carries her words around in your head. That shows me what kind of person you are."

Angie wanted to snort, but kept it in. "What kind of person does that make me, then?"

Fletcher spoke earnestly. "You feel things much more than most people."

"To my detriment, I suppose."

"No," Fletcher interjected. "It's a superpower. I hope you understand that."

Angie had nothing to say in return. She glanced at the clock on the wall, her heart buzzing. It was ten minutes till closing. For whatever reason, she had no idea if she wanted time to speed up or slow down. *Did she want this guy gone? Or to remain?*

Oh, but their conversation continued. Fletcher made sure it did. He spoke of his mother, who loved music but was unable to string more than two notes together. He spoke of his brother and sister, who had an ongoing feud about which Queen album was the best. Here, Angie interjected to say that Queen had no "great" albums— that only their compilation albums were worth listening to. Fletcher laughed uproariously and said Angie had taken the words directly from his sister's mouth. "My brother, however, would argue with you, tooth and nail, that *Sheer Heart Attack* has them all beat."

Angie chuckled, swirling her straw around and around her Manhattan glass. *Was there time to order another?* She glanced at the bartender, who'd begun to march around the tables, telling everyone it was closing time. Angie eyed Fletcher despairingly. Had she been a different sort of woman— a brave and modern woman in her twenties, perhaps— she might have asked him for one more drink, perhaps a nightcap in the bedroom attached to the bar itself.

But no! She could never. He was handsome, yes. Terribly so. He also made her feel special and wanted— something she'd thought, in her forties, was no longer possible. The cool thing, she knew, was to bid him goodnight almost immediately, leaving her only a curiosity in his mind. Perhaps he would find his way back to The Minty Green in the near future. Perhaps then, they could find their way to some kind of story.

It was better not to rush anything.

God, was this really happening? Was she actually flirting? Did she even really know how?

"Listen," Fletcher began, finishing up his whiskey on the rocks. "I know we just met."

I might vomit.

"But the thing is, I'm hosting an enormous event in August," Fletcher continued. "One that requires live music. One beautiful woman at the piano might not cut it, sadly. But a woman with a jazz ensemble? That's something we might be able to work with."

Angie's lips dropped open with surprise. Not only did he want to see her again, but he also wanted to hire her and a number of other working musicians for a real, probably high-paying gig. By the look of his suit and the choice of his whiskey (and the strangeness of his first name), it was clear to Angie that Fletcher was made of money.

"Do you have something like that out here on the east coast yet?" Fletcher asked.

Angie swallowed the lump in her throat. *Think, dummy.*

"I do," Angie lied, wanting to make herself readily available for something like this. "We're all east-coast jazz professionals. We normally practice in Bar Harbor, where I live."

"Ah." His eyes widened with a mix of surprise and intrigue. "I just love Bar Harbor."

"What's not to love about it?"

Fletcher laughed good-naturedly as he leafed a business card from his left-breast pocket. The card read:

Fletcher Baxter & Associates
   3457 S. Main Street
   Portland, ME
   Fletcher.Baxter@FBM.com

"And Associates?" Angie heard herself tease, surprising herself.

Fletcher continued to chuckle, as though anything that came out of Angie's mouth was gold to him and him alone. "That's right. My associates are the best associates of all the associates."

"That's good to hear," Angie quipped.

"Would you like to associate with me again?" Fletcher asked with a twinkle in his eye, playfulness in his words.

Angie's cheeks turned crimson. As she slipped the card into her purse, she forced her gaze back toward his handsome face. He seemed captivated by her.

"I wouldn't mind a brief association," Angie breathed.

"Good. Good." He said, repeating the word as though that finalized things. "Contact me this week, and I'll give you more details about the party itself. I cannot wait to tell my mother about your musical talents. She's going to fall in love."

He said it as though his mother wasn't the only one who planned to fall in love.

Again, he rapped the counter before splaying a twenty-dollar bill across it and bidding the bartender goodbye.

"Looking forward to seeing you again, Angie," Fletcher said before he disappeared through the shadows. "I think soon you'll have a whole lot more to play than sad love songs."

Chapter Six

"Abby and Hannah, Photography Specialists." Abby scribed the words on the top of a notepad with a shrug. "Boring. But it says what it is."

"It sounds like we're thirteen and selling polaroids in our backyard," Hannah joked.

Abby scrunched her nose and lifted her eyes toward the horizon of Frenchman Bay. Beyond, evening crept over the hazy waters, casting everything in a bluish light.

"A&H Photos," Hannah offered with a shrug. "Or, alternatively, H&A Photos." She gave Abby a cheeky smile and lifted her mango smoothie, the only thing that had stopped her endless overheating on this eighty-two-degree mid-July day.

Abby shook her head. "Maybe the name things doesn't work."

Nicole crept out from the foyer of the Keating House, wearing a tank top and a pair of shorts. A burn mark on her arm looked angry against her creamy skin.

"Mom! What did you do?" Abby cried.

"Oh, you know what it's like in the kitchen," Nicole replied with a wave of her hand. "I just got in the way of the piping hot skillet."

"Mom..." Abby groaned as she stood up to examine it. "Was it Luke? Did he do this to you?"

"No. Just one of the prep cooks," Nicole explained. "He nearly cried when it happened. Strangely, the pain made me laugh. Weird reaction, right?"

"I hope that I laugh all the way through labor and delivery," Hannah quipped.

Nicole scrunched her nose knowingly, having had two children herself. "You'll get through it. You're strong. That doesn't mean it doesn't absolutely hurt like heck. It does. But the body has a way of healing itself, thank goodness"

Nicole dropped down on the step beside Hannah, eyeing the smoothie and the laptop which was open, showing their newly created website for their photography business. The top two photographs featured Abby and the top part of Hannah, sans the pregnant belly. Already, Hannah had insisted that they retake the photograph after she lost more of the baby weight, as, in her eyes, you could make out the plumpness of her cheeks and the weight of her breasts. "Oh, come on. You look fantastic there," Abby had told her point-blank. "Nobody would guess that you're pregnant."

It had been one week since Nicole had officially hired them to manage the Keating Inn and Acadia Eatery social media strategy and website, and already, Abby and Hannah had fallen into the swing of things, taking upward of twenty-five photographs a day, scheduling five posts a day, answering online guest questions, and generally engaging in the online New England community. They'd also completely edited last week's engagement photographs for Candace and Godfrey and sent them along, receiving tremendous acclaim from Candace and her mother, Barb. (So far, Godfrey hadn't sent along so much as a "thank you." Probably, he was just grateful it was all over.)

As Nicole sat with Abby and Hannah, Abby scanned through the engagement photos, showing off what they'd done so far. Nicole was gobsmacked.

"Girls, you really have something here," she whispered.

Abby and Hannah laughed. It was a giddy laugh they'd recently taken on, one that translated just how unreal every-thing currently felt.

"Thanks. We just don't have a name for our business name yet. Hopefully, something will come to us sooner than later," Hannah said.

Nicole looked quizzical, her eyes to the glowing moon as it crested over the evening clouds. "It has to be memorable. Alive. Something that captures the light you create in the photographs themselves."

"Agreed," Abby said, snapping her fingers.

"Yes, but we can't exactly put 'something that captures the light you create in the photographs' in the website URL," Hannah joked.

Abby grimaced, her shoulders falling. On cue, her phone began to vibrate across her leg. She grabbed it, then whispered, "It's Candace!" and answered, putting on her front-desk voice.

"Good evening, Candace. It's Abby. Thank you for your tremendous feedback on the engagement photos."

Hannah watched Abby with bated breath, hardly able to trust their luck. She half-expected Candace to have called with news that they couldn't make the payment, after all— that they'd decided the photographs weren't up to their standards. That they wanted the Brooklyn Bridge, after all.

But instead, Abby's eyes widened with surprise. She dropped the phone back and pressed SPEAKER PHONE. Candace's New York City accent spouted out.

"—and they were like 'oh my God' and basically demanded

that we tell them, like, where we found you guys. So, I was like, ugh, okay. Okay. But I just have to check with you guys to make sure you are available first. So here I am, calling about that. Since it's an actual wedding and not, you know, engagement photos, I'm not worried about any repetitions between their photos and ours. Thank goodness."

"You never have to worry about that!" Abby cried. "We had a deal, and we always keep our word."

"Oh, you girls are just so sweet!" Candace said. "Listen. I have to run. But if you say you're available on July 23rd at such short notice, then I'll clear the way for them. They hired a truly heinous photographer based here in Brooklyn. I took one look at their website and literally died. I was like: you cannot do this to yourselves. These are the photos you're going to be looking at for the rest of your lives."

"We're putting the wedding on our calendar now," Abby assured her, gesturing for Hannah to write July 23rd down on the notepad.

Hannah wrote: **JULY 23— Wedding Photography for Crazy Friends of Candace?**

"And thank you for the recommendation," Abby said, as Nicole nodded furiously, happy she'd remembered to thank her. "We're a brand-new business and so grateful for your help."

"God, I'm just glad you exist!" Candace affirmed. "Godfrey and I's friends are so jealous. One of my friends literally burst into tears. She's one of the ones who got a photo in front of the Brooklyn Bridge. I'm like, basic much?"

Hannah was terribly grateful when Candace finally got off the phone. Abby and Hannah held the silence for a moment, staring down at Hannah's note on the pad of paper. It was Nicole who finally broke the silence, crying out, "Girls! Do you even know what this means?"

Abby and Hannah shook their head, still in shock.

"It means a whole, whole lot of money," Nicole told them. She splayed her hands out across her naked knees, showing off the massive burn on her arm. "Weddings are next-level."

The words echoed around Hannah's mind for the rest of the night.

Suddenly, she found herself on the road toward a brand-new life. Her baby playfully tapped its foot against the side of her stomach, wanting in on the joy. Hannah told Nicole and Abby about it, gesturing for them both to feel. Nicole and Abby both did, captivated for a moment at the feel of this miraculous creature within Hannah's body.

"It's like your baby wants to high-five us," Abby said, exuding with laughter.

"Oh God," Hannah joked. "I hope he or she isn't a high-five person. I won't know what to do with that."

Nicole and Abby burst into gut-belly laughter. It blanketed the rolling hills of the Keating Property and swelled across Frenchman Bay, echoing out from sailboat to sailboat. Through all that noise, Hannah's anxious mind stirred with thoughts like: *My baby and I will have food to eat. My baby and I will have a place to sleep. As long as I continue to work hard, our future will not burst apart into a million jagged pieces. I've got this.*

* * *

The next morning, Hannah awoke to a bouncing mattress.

So late in her pregnancy, exhaustion quivered in every bone of her body. She forced her eyes open to find her mother, Angie, seated on the side of her bed, bouncing only slightly and smiling at her as she cooed, "Hannah! Hannah! It's time to wake up."

Hannah groaned and closed her eyes again. "I need at least thirty more minutes of sleep."

"Not today, honey. You've got a doctor's appointment this morning. Had it in the calendar for two weeks now," Angie explained.

Hannah groaned even louder, enraged at herself for making such a stupid error. "I promised myself I wouldn't make any more morning appointments."

Angie chortled. "It starts at noon. You aren't breaking any promises whatsoever."

Hannah stood beneath the dribbling shower of their drab apartment, her eyes still closed as she slowly willed herself to wake up. In the kitchen, on the other side of the bathroom door, Angie played Billy Joel on the little stereo. It sounded like she opened and slammed every single cabinet, looking for something. If Hannah closed her eyes for a split second and played pretend, she could imagine herself at age fifteen, showering at the Chicago apartment she'd grown up in. Maybe, if she opened the bathroom door, she'd discover her mother and father, both doing the crossword as they sipped their coffee. Maybe, she could go back in time.

Given the humidity and the enormity of her stomach, dresses seemed the only way forward. She donned a yellow one she'd picked out at a local second-hand shop and brought a brush through her hair. When she returned to the kitchen, four eggs sizzled in a skillet, and her mother moved her hips around to the Billy Joel beats. It wasn't the past. It was the present. But there was enough joy to it. It would do.

After eggs, Angie drove Hannah to the doctor's office, where Hannah propped herself up on a gurney in the room as the ultrasound technician poured cold gel on her belly and began the scan. She watched in amazement as her little baby appeared on the screen. She'd requested not to learn the gender, choosing instead to believe in the "power of surprise." The technician was still just as surprised about that as she'd been the first time.

"Are you really sure? I can tell you right now," she told Hannah, yet again.

The technician cleared Hannah and her baby, maintaining that "both mama and baby look healthy as ever." Hannah resented when people called her "mama" but still glowed with happiness at the status of her baby. She then waddled out of the office next to her mother, already staggering with hunger. Angie took one look at her and sensed it.

"The eggs weren't enough, huh?"

"What? Two eggs? That was like, an hour ago."

"All right." Angie cackled and removed her car keys from her purse. "Let's hit that salad place on the way back."

Hannah wrinkled her nose. "I'm pretty sure 'mama and baby' want French fries and a grilled cheese or clubhouse sandwich."

Angie groaned. "You want to go to the diner? Again?"

Hannah's smile split her face open.

"Okay. Okay." Angie rolled her eyes. "But we're ordering a fruit cup."

"Fine," Hannah groaned.

By one that afternoon, Angie and Hannah sat at their familiar booth at the diner. Outside, July heat steamed the pavement so that a mirage formed on the far end of the parking lot. Hannah ordered herself a strawberry milkshake, while Angie stuck with water and a Diet Coke. After that, they ordered a grilled cheese, a club sandwich, French fries, a fruit cup, and a side salad. Hannah would do her best to eat as much of the "nutritional crap" as possible. For the baby's sake, of course.

After they ordered, Angie sipped her Diet Coke and burst into a smile.

"What's gotten into you?" Hannah demanded.

Angie shivered. "I've just gotten asked to perform at a huge event in August. Big money, Hannah. Big."

Hannah's eyes widened. *Was this the beginning of their good luck streak? Would it ever run dry?*

"I just have to put together a jazz ensemble because I kind of already said I have one," Angie explained. "I have auditions set up for this Saturday. Already, ten people have written me about coming along. Two drummers. A trombonist. Several trumpeters. A saxophonist..." She counted them out on her fingers and shrugged. "I had no idea there were so many musicians in the area. I'm over the moon!"

Hannah's heart opened wide enough to experience the full breadth of her mother's joy. "That's fantastic, Mom. Really. What's the event?"

Angie shrugged. "Some rich guy based in Portland. I guess people like that have to throw parties. To impress their friends. Who knows?"

"Who knows," Hannah echoed. She then added, "I wanted to tell you last night. Abby and I've been hired to photograph a wedding on the 23rd. We're going to ask for upward of four thousand dollars."

Angie's jaw dropped. She squeezed Hannah's wrist as her eyes filled with tears. "I'm so damn proud of you two."

Hannah shrugged. "It feels like the opportunity just kind of fell out of the air."

"That doesn't account for the huge amount of effort you and Abby have put in the past couple of weeks," Angie affirmed. "You should be proud."

"It's overwhelming," Hannah whispered, breathless. She swiped a stray tear from her cheek, cursing herself and her pregnancy hormones. "Ah, but Abby and I still don't have a name for our business."

Angie furrowed her brow, her eyes to the ceiling of the diner. On the speaker, the B52's "Love Shack" romped along. Angie's smile widened from ear to ear.

"No, Mom," Hannah shot out, already reading her mother's mind.

"Come on, honey. Love Shack! Love Shack Photography! It's adorable," Angie said. "You're Bar Harbor-based wedding, engagement, graduation, and special event photographers. You put love into everything you do. Give me one good reason why 'Love Shack Photography' isn't a good name? Come on, honey. I'm all ears."

Although it was terribly difficult, Hannah had to admit it. Her mother had a point.

Chapter Seven

As Angie drove back from The Minty Green that Friday morning after a late-night Thursday shift, Heather sent out a mass text to all Harvey-Keating relatives, Luke, Angie, and Hannah, suggesting a "big celebratory barbecue."

HEATHER: I've been gone for too gosh-darn long. I'm ready to celebrate summer with all of you. I hope you haven't forgotten all about me yet.

Angie laughed to herself, tossing her phone into the passenger seat as it exploded with messages. At the next red light, she silenced it, dropping her head against the car seat headrest and watching the light. The previous night had been a whirlwind, one that had left her heavy with exhaustion yet buzzing with adrenaline.

Fletcher Baxter had returned to The Minty Green.

Throughout her set, he'd watched her. Angie had been conscious of his watching throughout, careful not to touch a single incorrect note. Nobody, not even her ex-husband, had analyzed her musical abilities so acutely in many, many years.

Maybe not since music school. It both thrilled her and terrified her.

Afterward, Fletcher sat with her for a nightcap. As they'd already agreed that Angie's band would perform for his August party, their conversation fell to other, more enlightening things. They'd discussed poetry, music, books they loved, and books they hated. Angie's ears had grown to crave his laugh.

And yet again, she'd dared herself to ask him into the back bedroom for an additional nightcap; yet again, she'd failed to meet that dare. Perhaps it had been fear, both of him and of losing out on the opportunity to play at his party. Regardless, just after midnight, he'd again disappeared into the darkness— and left Angie only with her reckless daydreaming.

Daydreaming was so nourishing and painful, all at once. She'd forgotten that.

* * *

Angie arrived home around noon to a sloppy apartment. Excited by their growing businesses and their new prospects, both Hannah and Angie had thrown themselves into their new dreams— and, with that, thrown around their sweatshirts, blankets, towels, books, and everything in between. Angie laughed to herself, thinking that the apartment looked a whole lot more like an apartment shared between friends rather than mother and daughter. But there was a beauty in that, too.

Hannah appeared from the darkness of her bedroom around twelve-thirty, yawning and tripping over her feet. She found Angie elbow-deep in suds, scrubbing the dishes and listening to a podcast about the current state of the music industry in her headphones. Angie grinned and shrugged her headphones off.

"Good morning, sleepy head."

Hannah laughed and dropped into a kitchen chair. "It looks so good in here."

"I just couldn't take the mess anymore," Angie said.

"I'm so sorr—"

"It's both of our faults." Angie shrugged as she wiped her hands on the nearest towel. "It's been an overwhelming time. Between searching for Wendy's care facility, awaiting the new baby, building up the new band, and building your photography business? I'm frankly surprised we find time to sleep at night."

Hannah laughed, checking her phone as she yawned again. "Heather's back?"

"You up for a big, old-fashioned Harvey family barbecue?" Angie asked with her hands on her hips.

"I'll say what I always say before these things," Hannah said, her eyes sparkling. "I can always eat."

Around five-thirty, Angie and Hannah piled into Angie's car and drove through the classic small-town American streets of downtown Bar Harbor, which was still mostly decorated for the Fourth of July. As they drove, several people waved in greeting, whether or not they knew Angie and Hannah. Unconsciously, both Angie and Hannah waved back.

"Gosh, I hardly realized I just did that," Hannah said, slapping her thigh. "My Chicago friends wouldn't recognize me."

"Yeah," Angie teased. "You're just too gosh-darn friendly these days. You better knock it out."

Hannah stuck out her tongue. She then dropped her head back contemplatively as she added, "By the way. I hate admitting this, but Abby absolutely adored the idea for 'Love Shack Photography.' She said it's memorable. We already have the website up and running. Abby even wants to make business cards. I mean, business cards are pretty insufferable, right?"

Angie giggled, remembering the business card from one Fletcher Baxter, which still burned a hole in her wallet. "I think it's just how things work in the business world. What do I know? I was in the same band for decades. Your father did all our business strategizing."

Hannah made a soft sound in the base of her throat. Angie made another mental note not to bring up Hannah's father. It was too tender of a subject.

The Keating House appeared in the front window of the car, a staggering beauty of a house upon the hill nearest the Keating Inn and Acadia Eatery, with a splendorous view of Frenchman Bay and the Acadia Mountain up above it. Angie took the snaking driveway up toward the house and parked. From where they sat, they could see several of the Harvey members through the windows, making their way through the house, talking excitedly. From the side porch, smoke billowed from the barbecue.

Suddenly, Abby burst from the door, waving both hands like a child. Hannah laughed and muttered, "What a nerd!" before shoving the passenger door open. Abby hustled for her, giving her support as she exited the car.

"You won't believe this. The website already had seventy-three views today," Abby told her. "I think the search engine optimization is working. That, and Candace's support of us. She shared our site on her social media."

"What!" Hannah looked incredulous. "I can't believe how willing she is to support us."

"She must really hate the Brooklyn Bridge," Abby quipped.

Angie followed after the two of them, carrying a bottle of wine she'd nabbed from her own fridge— probably a terrible grape, one that Heather would attempt to hide behind the other bottles at the party. Heather would never purposefully describe the wine as "awful." Her palate just came from a different class, is all. Angie couldn't fault her for that, she supposed.

Still, it had seemed inappropriate not to bring something to the party, especially since the Harveys had done so much for Angie and Hannah over the past half-year.

To Angie's tremendous surprise, Luke popped out of the kitchen first to greet Angie and Hannah. He wore his traditional barbecue apron, which read "Kiss the Cook," and had a bit of soot on his cheek from the barbecue coal.

"You made it!" He looked genuinely pleased. Angie couldn't help but match his smile. He beckoned for them to enter the kitchen, grabbing her wine, and crying, "Oh, I love this one. I always get this kind when Heather isn't around." He winked at Angie, who felt entirely connected to this human— her little brother. He just got her without explanation. That was a rare thing.

"Hi!" Heather stepped back inside from the porch. She was sun-kissed from her time away, effervescent, and happy from conversations with her daughters and endless bottles of expensive wine. "Angie, it's so good to see you. You too, Hannah. Abby was just telling us all about 'Love Shack Photography.' What a clever name!"

"Mom came up with it." Hannah was quick to point out.

Heather's eyes widened. "I'm not surprised. Angie. You've got a wild creative streak up that sleeve of yours."

This was high praise from a woman who'd made her career as a fantasy YA writer. Angie's cheeks burned with a mix of embarrassment and gratefulness.

They headed out toward the porch, which wrapped around the Keating House and featured a large picnic table, recently extended to account for the enormity of their ever-growing clan. At the head of the table sat Casey and Grant, who hovered over the architectural plans for the brand-new Keating House, which Casey had designed in the back part of the Keating Property. They'd broken ground that spring and would hopefully finish by the time winter hit. To Angie, who knew next to nothing about architecture, this seemed a tight turnaround.

"We've got burgers, chicken, homemade onion rings..." Luke began to list the food items, waving his spatula around like an excited kid. "Basically, enough food to feed several horses."

"That means there's nowhere near enough," Nicole joked from where she sat near Casey, lifting a glass of wine toward Angie and Hannah in greeting.

"Can I do anything to help?" Angie asked, feeling out of her element.

"Nothing in the slightest," Luke replied. "Except keep me company by the grill."

Hannah and Abby sat alongside one another at the picnic table, Abby with a glass of wine and Hannah with a glass of sparkling water. Abby propped up her computer and gestured toward something, probably the numbers for their website. Nicole teased them to "give it up," that it was Friday evening and "time to party." Abby stuck her tongue out to her mother and said, "We're trying to build our future!"

"How's it going lately?" Luke spoke quietly, just for Angie to hear. It pulled her from her reverie.

"Oh. Gosh." Angie wasn't sure where to start. "I'm fighting for my life, trying to make enough money for Mom's memory care facility and the upcoming baby. Plus rent." Panic swirled in her gut.

Luke flipped over several pink burgers, showing their graying other sides. He muttered, "Can't even imagine what that must feel like, Ang."

"I know finding that money for Mom isn't any easier for you," Angie pointed out.

Luke grimaced, turning his eyes toward Heather, the woman he so loved. Heather had far and away more money than either of them. *Why didn't he ask her for help?*

It was as though Luke could hear Angie's thoughts.

"Our relationship is still pretty new," Luke continued to mutter, his eyes focused on the burgers. "It was a difficult thing, even convincing her that she was ready to have a relationship again after her husband's death."

Angie grimaced. "I can't even imagine."

"We're happier than ever. But I don't want to complicate things with big money talks. Two grand a month is no small thing. And I'd rather it come from me. From her children."

"Me too." Angie's heart swelled with love for her brother. After a pause, she added, "I think I'm just too proud. Too stubborn."

Luke laughed. "Maybe that runs in the family."

Angie tilted her head, remembering the stubbornness of her adopted father, Chester. Although theirs had been a complicated relationship, he was still the only father she'd ever known. She lifted her eyes toward the evening sky and tried to speak to him, wherever he was. *Thank you for all you taught me. I know that you did your best.*

A little while later, the Harvey-Keating clan, plus all extended family and friends, sat around the picnic table for burgers, grilled chicken, crabs, homemade onion rings, watermelon, and potato salad. Angie sat next to her daughter and across from her little brother, falling in love with the wild conversation, the blissful laughter, and the energy of the big, old house.

Over crabs, the subject of Hannah's baby's future name came up.

"I'm taking suggestions," Hannah said, laughing.

"Okay. I got it." Luke looked conspiratorial. "What about Jabba the Hut?"

Everyone cackled. Hannah pretended to take it seriously, even writing it down on her "baby name list" on her phone.

"It has a real ring to it," she told him.

Luke snapped his fingers. "That's what I thought."

"Oh, come on, Luke." Heather wrapped a beautiful, manicured hand around Luke's wrist. "I know. What if you name him Charles? Charlie for short. Isn't that adorable?"

"And if it's a girl, she could still be called Charlie," Casey pointed out from down the table.

"Ugh. I don't know," Hannah replied. "I've had complicated experiences with people named Charlie."

"Uh oh. I remember that when I was naming my son," Nicole said with a laugh. "My ex-husband, Michael, was fixated on the name Vincent. But that was the name of the only boy who'd ever broken my heart!"

"Oh no. There's no way. Imagine saying that name over and over again," their cousin, Brittany Keating, said, wrinkling her nose. "Did he fight you on it?"

"Tooth and nail!" Nicole cried, locking eyes with Brittany. "But that's how Michael always was."

"You got out of it, though," Brittany pointed out.

"Miraculously," Nicole added with a wry laugh. "I'm sure he made me pay for it in some other, small way."

Nicole and Brittany had something in common. They'd both married and had children with very manipulative and cruel men. You could feel their connection across the table, over the cooling burgers and the goop of the potato salad.

Casey and Grant discussed their own children's names: Melody and Donnie.

"I can't remember fighting about them," Grant said.

Casey all-out chuckled. "Are you kidding me? We fought about girl names for weeks. You wanted something atrocious. What was it?"

"I don't believe that at all. Melody is a perfect name," Grant shot back.

"I know that very well," Casey returned with a sniff. "Gosh, I wish I could think of the silly name you wanted. Was it something like Zoey?" She furrowed her brow as Grant dropped his eyes to the table.

"Uh oh. He suddenly remembered," Heather said, snapping her fingers.

"I did not," Grant muttered, clearly lying.

"Grant! Come on." Casey pressed her hands together, praying. "Please. Tell us. Let me walk down memory lane for a minute."

"All right!" Grant howled. "It was Bowie."

Casey burst into reckless giggles. The rest of the clan followed suit. Even Angie nearly spit out her potato salad as tears fell from her eyes.

"What?" Grant demanded, aghast. "I was going through a serious David Bowie phase."

"David Bowie is fantastic, Grant. Totally," Nicole tried to help him out.

But Casey wouldn't let him off the hook. "Our poor, darling Melody. I'm so glad I protected her."

Grant groaned but soon burst into laughter, as well. He then lifted his eyes toward Angie, the quietest one at the table. "What about you, Ang? Did you almost name Hannah anything really creative? I need your help since you're a musician yourself."

Angie bit hard on her lower lip, eyeing her gorgeous daughter. Hannah's cheeks blushed pink.

"Actually, it was pretty easy to name Hannah," Angie said, quiet enough that everyone had to dip their heads forward to hear. "I named her after my mother, Hannah, who died when I was quite young."

Her heart swelled with an ache that had never gone away, one that meant that, forever, she would miss that woman. That woman who, it turned out, had adopted her. How insane that her adoptive mother had wanted her for who she was and all she was, despite the fact that she was someone else's toddler.

Suddenly, Heather lifted her glass of wine, her ocean-blue eyes locked on Angie's. "I think we'd better make a toast to Hannah, our Hannah's namesake. Don't you think?"

"To Hannah," Nicole affirmed, raising her glass.

Together, the entire crew raised their glasses. Angie blinked as quickly as a hummingbird's wings. Softly, she joined their voices as they said, "To Hannah," and drank. Her heart swelled as her eyes searched the horizon of Frenchman Bay. It had been a long time since she'd felt her adopted mother's love. Maybe, for a brief moment, she felt it right there at that table.

Chapter Eight

S aturday afternoon, Luke stepped out from the Acadia Eatery kitchen in stained chef's whites, his chef hat crumpled and his cheeks pink from the harsh steam from the lunch rush. He spread his arms out wide, greeting Angie like a cult leader. And then he said, "Angie? The space is all yours. You have four hours."

Angie stood beside the baby grand piano and the drum set along the wall of the Acadia Eatery's dining area, her heart throttling. Just as Luke and Nicole had promised, the Acadia Eatery would cease operations between lunch and dinner to allow her time for auditions. Already, several of her musician guests awaited her in the foyer of the Keating Inn, their fingers fluttering over the keys of their instruments and their eyes buggy with expectation. No matter how old you were or how many times you'd played professionally, auditions hardly got any easier. Angie knew that well.

Abby stood in the doorway between the Acadia Eatery and the Keating Inn foyer, a clipboard pressed against her stomach. Upon that clipboard, Angie had written out the list of people auditioning. Abby had agreed to send each of them into the Eatery in the order Angie had written them, operating the entire affair like a much more professional jazz ensemble. It was best to start as you meant to go on, Angie felt. Abby had wholeheartedly agreed.

Suddenly, Hannah bustled into the Acadia Eatery, her cheeks flushed and the fabric of her dress jostling around her pregnant belly.

"Honey! You made it." Angie had initially asked her incredibly musical daughter to assist with the audition process but hadn't assumed it would work out.

Hannah collapsed in the chair Angie had set up, fanning herself with a flat hand. "I thought about my own audition processes," Hannah offered, puffing out her cheeks. "And how unfair I always found them to be when there was only one person present."

Angie nodded, understanding Hannah's point. The audition seemed to matter more and hold more respect if an extra pair of ears gave insight. Angie grabbed another chair and positioned it next to Hannah as Hannah removed a pad of paper and a pen from her backpack.

"Notes," Hannah said, flipping open the pad.

"Good idea," Angie replied, grabbing her own stack of scrap paper. She then turned toward Abby and gave a nod of affirmation. "We're ready for our first musician."

Abby disappeared and was soon replaced with a forty-two-year-old saxophonist named Marvin. Marvin had a bright patch of carrot-colored hair and wore a truly heinous lime-green sweater.

"Hi," he said, adjusting himself on the chair set up near the piano bench.

"Hi," Hannah and Angie replied in unison. Angie prayed that Marvin, nor the others, could sense just how nervous she and Hannah were. It was a funny thing, being on the other side of the process.

Marvin blinked at them. They blinked back.

Angie started, realizing she was running this show. "Yes. Well. Marvin." She smacked her thighs lightly. "My name is Angie, and I'm a professional pianist, originally from the Midwest. I moved to Bar Harbor earlier this year and am finally following my instincts and putting together a jazz ensemble. We'll play jazz standards, of course, and improv all together, with the hopes of putting together our own songs."

Marvin's grin seemed electric. "I have to admit. The idea of creating brand-new songs with a collection of people thrills me." He leaned forward conspiratorially as he added, "I can only play 'Fly Me to the Moon' so many times, you know?"

Angie laughed. "Oh, boy. I know that all too well."

Marvin placed his lips on the reed of his instrument, closed his eyes, tensed his cheeks, and began to play. Already, Angie sensed the ease he had with his instrument, as though he'd been born with the metal beneath his fingers. The tone of his saxophone was clear and thick and soulful, the perfect sort of thing for Angie's ensemble. In fact, to Angie's ears, he was far better than the saxophonist she and her ex-husband had performed with back in Chicago.

When Marvin finished, both Hannah and Angie clapped, which wasn't exactly a common sight in an audition. Marvin blinked at them, his cheeks growing pink. Angie's clapping staggered to a halt. Beside her, Hannah scribbled out: "**HE IS THE BOMB**" on her notepad.

"Thank you so much for coming in today, Marvin," Angie breathed. She sounded like a teenager with a crush.

Marvin laughed. "Thank you for having me!"

Angie leaned forward, her eyes in slits. "Do you have other bands you're playing with here in Bar Harbor?"

Marvin shook his head. "Tell you the truth. I've lived half

my life in Portland. Only just made it out to Bar Harbor this past autumn and haven't found any ensembles quite right for me."

Angie's eyes widened. It was nourishing to find someone with a similar story with a similar need. "We'll be in contact soon," she told Marvin as he stood up, giving her a childish grin.

After Marvin, a twenty-something saxophonist with curly hair that fell all the way down his back stepped through the doorway. It took Angie little more than ten seconds to understand that he'd just found the saxophone in the back closet of his parents' place and decided to screech-practice until he made some kind of sound. Naturally, he wasn't suited for the caliber of jazz performance Angie needed— but she told him to take heart.

"You should look into lessons!" Angie said excitedly, grateful to discover a younger person who was still interested in learning more about music. So often, she felt the world had decided to move on without music, underfunding school programs and pushing sports instead.

"Yeah..." Hannah sounded doubtful beside her, scribbling out: "**OMG**" on her pad of paper.

The twenty-something didn't look entirely displeased. Instead, he jumped up and said that he was "inspired" by eighties tracks and that his biggest dream was to play the saxophone solo from "Baker Street" by the end of the summer. When Angie explained that "Baker Street" was actually a song from the 1970s, he simply shrugged and blared his saxophone again.

"All right. I think we're ready for our next musician," Angie joked as the twenty-something disappeared.

"He was a trip," Hannah said, shaking her head. She bent down to whisper to her pregnant belly, "I promise to keep you safe from people like him."

Angie swatted her daughter playfully on the shoulder as their third musician came through— a trumpeter named Ashlee who'd majored in music twenty years ago and had never managed to do much with it since.

Afterward came a steady stream of musicians: two drummers who weren't half-bad; two more trumpeters; another saxophonist; a bassist; a clarinetist; another pianist, whom Angie asked to leave immediately; and a trombonist.

Three hours after they'd begun, Hannah and Angie had locked down most of their choices. Ashlee was their trumpeter; the only bassist, Trevor, was good enough; Marvin, naturally, was their saxophonist; Gregory would play the trombone, at least for now, until Hannah could join the ensemble.

"I still don't feel good about our drummers," Angie said, chewing at the edge of her pen.

Hannah groaned. "I know. That first one lost the tempo a few times."

"That's rule one for drumming," Angie said.

Suddenly, Abby stepped back through the doorway, waving her clipboard. "Hey! Another guy just came in. He said he's late but still wants to audition."

"Tell me he's a drummer!" Angie cried.

Abby grinned. "How did you know?"

Angie and Hannah locked eyes. Hannah crossed her first and second fingers and shook them, whispering, "If he's no good, I'm sure my baby can take over the drumming. He or she is really pounding away in there."

Angie chortled. "You think your baby will be born with the dexterity to hold onto drumsticks?"

Hannah grimaced. "Are you suggesting that your grandchild isn't capable of greatness? That isn't very grandmotherly of you."

A stoic-looking man with burly shoulders and the long, lean muscles of a typical drummer appeared, his drumsticks stuffed into his back pocket. He had a thin black beard and high cheek-bones, and he wore a black t-shirt and a pair of baggy jeans. Angie guessed he was somewhere around her age, maybe mid to late forties. He looked as though he hadn't found a reason to smile in years.

"Hi, there," Angie said, glancing again at her list of musicians. "I don't have you on my list. Can you introduce yourself? Tell us a bit about yourself?"

The man sat at the drum set, adjusting the chair. When he spoke, his voice was masculine and sure of itself, yet not brash or arrogant in the slightest.

"Hi. My name is Paul Dappler." He wiggled his shoulders, loosening himself up. "I'm a drummer originally from Boston. I came up to Bar Harbor about two years ago, after early retire-ment. Back in Boston, I played in a number of bands across many genres. Rock. Punk. Even a metal band, once."

Hannah laughed. "Metal?"

Paul gave her the sneakiest of smiles. "Not exactly my favorite style of music, but the drumming was so difficult that it made the experience fun."

"That's what I wanted to say," Hannah offered hurriedly. "Metal and punk drummers are usually killer."

Paul shrugged. "I'm more interested in jazz these days."

"Why's that?" Angie asked, cocking her head.

Paul's chocolate brown eyes were soulful. To Angie, they were the eyes of a musician.

"There's just so much more room for being playful in jazz," he said. "Once you feel the music with someone, you can create magic together."

Angie could hardly breathe. She swallowed the lump in her throat and eyed her scrap paper. If she looked up at Paul's gorgeous chocolate eyes again, she thought she might cry.

"Sounds good, Paul," Angie said to her pen, her voice straining. "Why don't you show us what you've got?"

Paul was a real musician, the sort you don't come across so often. The way he played the drums was organic and nuanced, his drumsticks flowing across the cymbals and high hats and bass drums easily, without any hesitation. It was clear that he'd spent hundreds and hundreds of hours practicing so that the drum set was more an extension of his body than anything else.

When Paul finished, he opened his eyes wider and peered across the set at Hannah and Angie. Both were silent with surprise. Paul stood and shoved his drumsticks into his back pocket, still stoic.

Angie urged herself to say something. Anything.

"Wow," she finally said.

"Seriously," Hannah shot out.

One corner of Paul's lips curved toward his ear. *Was this the only sort of smile he could manage?*

"I think I speak for both of us when I say you're hired," Angie said, her heart pounding.

"I'm grateful," Paul returned. *Was that all he could say?*

"Do you have a card or something? A way we could reach out to you with information. We'll probably start rehearsal next week," Angie continued.

"I don't have a card, no," Paul told her with a shrug.

"Thank goodness," Hannah muttered.

Paul said nothing. Angie stood and stepped toward him, her nostrils flared as she took in the oaky texture of his cologne. She passed him her pen and scrap paper and said, "Write down your number and email?"

He bent to do it, eyeing a note that Angie had written about the twenty-something saxophonist. "Has a good heart and is very optimistic."

"I know you didn't write that about me," Paul joked as he passed the paper back to Angie.

Angie laughed nervously. "We had a young man here today

who'd probably picked up the saxophone three or four times in his life."

Paul gave her that secretive smile again. "I wish I'd been blessed with the kind of courage it takes to go into an audition without knowing how to play your instrument."

"Ditto!" Hannah called from her chair.

Paul and Angie held one another's gaze for a moment. Angie's tongue felt heavy and scratchy, like sandpaper.

"I'll be in contact soon," Angie explained.

"Sounds good," Paul said, shoving his drumsticks back into his pocket. He then lifted a firm hand to wave as he stepped back through the hallway.

Angie collapsed back on the chair beside her daughter, aghast. Hannah poked her with a sharp elbow, her eyebrows dancing.

"What?" Angie demanded.

"Come on. I saw the way you looked at him."

Angie stiffened. "I like good musicians."

Hannah grumbled inwardly. "You like dark, mysterious strangers."

"Oh, I do not."

"You little liar," Hannah said with a sneaky smile.

Angie hadn't yet told her daughter about her true crush, the handsome stranger named Fletcher. That was her little secret, something she could nourish during her late nights at The Minty Green. Eventually, she would work up the nerve to ask for that night cap. Eventually, she would honor her feelings.

When Angie and Hannah emerged from the Acadia Eatery dining room, they found Abby with her elbows on the front desk, circling locations on a Bar Harbor map for a newly arrived couple. The couple was in their twenties, both artfully dressed in hipster-chic clothing. They looked straight from the glossy pages of a magazine.

"Hannah! I'd like you to meet our clients for this upcoming

wedding weekend!" Abby cried. "Victor? Natalie? This is my business partner, Hannah."

Natalie and Victor turned to take in the full view of pregnant Hannah.

"Goodness!" Natalie breathed. "Candace mentioned that one of you was pregnant."

"Not long now," Hannah affirmed, using a voice Angie hardly recognized. It sounded like her "business persona." "But I'll be just fine for your wedding next week. Abby and I have worked out a good system so that I don't have to be on my feet all the time."

"Brilliant," Natalie returned kindly.

"Oh. This is my mother, Angie," Hannah added.

"Hello, Angie," Natalie greeted her. "Are you a photographer as well?"

"No, I'm afraid not," Angie replied with a soft smile.

"She's a brilliant musician," Hannah explained. "We were just auditioning people to be in her newly-founded jazz ensemble."

Natalie's eyes bugged out. She glanced at her fiancé, muttering, "Babe..."

Victor arched his brow. After an awkward pause, he added, "She's in a tizzy because we don't have any music arranged for the dinner portion of our reception."

"Just a DJ for dancing," Natalie explained in a whiny voice. "And everyone knows DJ music is trashy during dinner."

Victor flung his hands into the air. Angie could practically hear the anxious screaming of his mind.

"Mom would love to perform," Hannah interjected.

"Oh gosh. It's such short notice," Natalie breathed, clearly panicked. She looked at Angie as though she was her knight in shining armor.

"Mom can put it together in a week," Hannah assured her, nudging Angie with that sharp elbow of hers. "Right, Mom?"

"We have the budget for it," Natalie assured Angie.

Victor looked as though he wanted to vomit. But all Angie could think about was the ever-approaching payment to her mother's memory care clinic, Hannah's baby, the rent that needed to be paid, and the food that needed to be eaten. Even if this meant throwing together a band as quickly as possible, practicing five hours a day, and putting together a ragtag set, how could she possibly turn down such an enticing offer?

"We'd love to be a part of your special day," Angie heard herself say, her grin widening. "What a wonderful idea."

Chapter Nine

The local dollar store was off the beaten path and something the Harvey Sisters probably knew nothing about. Hannah and Angie, on the other hand, frequented the place, grabbing cleaning supplies, some snacks, office supplies, and anything else that struck their fancy— each item, just one dollar. It was there, on the Monday before Natalie and Victor's wedding, that Hannah discovered the two massive calendars, each for one buck each.

"We need these, Mom." Hannah opened up the calendar to show off the enormity of the second half of July. "Your band was only just formed, and already, you have two gigs lined up. That, on top of your gigs at The Minty Green, plus my work with Love Shack Photography? We're slammed. We have to stay organized."

Angie smirked. She had a big bag of candy under her arm and carried a plastic bucket, which they'd told themselves would make them mop the apartment more often.

"And us needing these calendars has nothing to do with the fact that they're cat-themed?" Angie asked.

Hannah dropped her head down to re-assess the adorable cats in July 2022. In one calendar, a cat hid under a bookshelf, sleeping on a big green pillow. In another, a cat snuck behind a plant, its big eyes glowing from just behind a leaf.

"Nothing at all," Hannah affirmed. "Although I have to warn you. Saying they're not adorable is sacrilegious."

"And where do you suggest we hang them?" Angie asked with a funny laugh. "We're running out of space in our little hideaway, my love."

"We'll figure something out," Hannah told her. "And the way I think of it, the more organized we become, the closer we get to reaching our goal of getting the heck out of there. Less wall space right now means more wall space later."

Angie tossed her head back. "I don't know if that math adds up."

"Mom, we've been over this. At the dollar store, math is the easiest thing of all," Hannah shot back.

Back at home, a very pregnant Hannah stood wide-legged in just a sports bra and some ratty-looking underwear, smacking two nails into the kitchen wall. She then hung the calendars, adjusting them side by side so that the plant-cat and the pillow-cat sat there right next to the breakfast table. She then took a big, fat permanent marker and marked the following Saturday on both calendars like so:

NATALIE AND VICTOR'S BIG WEDDING EXTRAVAGANZA

She then circled the words with seven-dollar signs, which looked silly and stupid, but she was too excited to care. When Angie walked in and assessed Hannah's work, she coughed with laughter.

"Wow. I don't think there's any chance I'll forget the big day," Angie teased.

Hannah then lifted a page to produce August. After a long sigh, she dropped her marker on AUGUST 22 and wrote:

BABY'S BIG DUE DATE

"Phew," Angie breathed.

"Phew," Hannah echoed.

They were wordless for a moment, each eyeing that big whopper of a day— both thrilled and worried. Angie then stood in front of the calendar and wrote on AUGUST 15:

WENDY'S MOVE-IN DAY

"Ugh," Hannah moaned.

"It's okay. We can do this," Angie affirmed, clicking the end of the permanent marker with her thumb.

A text buzzed through Hannah's phone.

ABBY: I can't wait until our business can be full-time.

ABBY: I'm so done with the front desk!

ABBY: You won't believe what these guests just complained about.

ABBY: It's too sunny in their room! They literally have too good of a view of Frenchman Bay and the gorgeous sunlight over the water! When I asked them about the (well-made) curtains, they simply said they'd prefer a darker room for better sleeping. I wanted to say, glad you came all the way here from Oklahoma to be unconscious.

Hannah snickered as she read Abby's outraged texts, dropping onto a kitchen chair. Angie yanked open a bag of chips they'd grabbed at the dollar store and selected a triangular-shaped cheese-flavoring and ate it daintily, her eyes still on the calendars.

"So, Mom." Hannah placed her phone back down and grabbed a chip for herself. "Did you hear back from all the musicians?"

Angie nodded, her smile blossoming. "Everyone's in and ready to rehearse, starting tomorrow."

Hannah rapped her knuckles on the table. "That's what I like to hear."

Angie closed her eyes and ate another chip. She looked utterly blissful, at peace, just as she had two days before, as that immeasurably talented drummer had ripped across the drum set, producing a sound that Hannah had very rarely heard.

This led Hannah to ask the question that had been burning in the back of her mind all summer long, one that she knew needed to be asked. As she took the plunge into motherhood, she wanted her mother to have the strength to build a new life, as well.

"Mom?"

"Hmm?" Angie didn't bother to open her eyes.

"Have you, um. Have you sent Dad the divorce papers yet?"

Silence. Angie's eyes opened into slits. Hannah stared down at her recently painted fingernails, praying that the words hadn't cut her mother too deeply.

Angie lifted herself from the kitchen table and ruffled through the pile of papers on the counter, the one made up of bills they hadn't yet paid and notices they'd decided to ignore. Beneath it all sat the divorce papers, which Hannah's father had sent sometime in May. Angie splayed them across the kitchen table, her eyes dampening.

"I want to sign them. I really do," Angie whispered. "But there's something holding me back."

Hannah nodded, only half-understanding. Her father had been terribly cruel to her mother— so harsh that she'd made up her mind to move halfway across the continent and build a new life.

"It's difficult to explain," Angie breathed. "I suppose it's like finding an old sweater you used to love in the back of your closet. You know instinctively that it no longer fits you. That it's filled with holes and maybe even moths. Maybe there's even a snake somewhere in there, ready to bite you. But gosh, you have such good memories in that sweater. How could you just throw it all away?"

Hannah's eyes filled with tears. Inwardly, she cursed her pregnancy hormones, yet knew, also, that it was so much bigger than that. As an only child, her parents had been her entire world. Hearing her mother speak this truth about the feelings she harbored for her father tore her apart inside.

Hannah would have bet a thousand dollars that her father felt the same.

But sometimes, there was no going back.

Hannah splayed a hand over her mother's and whispered, "But you know what they say about old, hole-filled, snake-infested sweaters, don't you?"

Angie shook her head delicately.

"When you finally throw them away, you can go shopping for brand-new sweaters," Hannah finished. "Ones that actually fit."

A single tear drifted down Angie's cheek. Silence filled the tiny kitchen. As Angie opened her lips to speak, Angie's phone buzzed on the other side of the table. Hannah laughed good-naturedly, saying, "Maybe it's that handsome drummer asking you out."

Angie's laughter twinkled like music. She grabbed her phone, read the message, and immediately turned beet-red.

"I knew it," Hannah said. "It's him. Paul, the drummer. The hottest and most mysterious man around."

But when Angie lifted her eyes toward Hannah's, Hannah recognized that her mother had a secret. There was a glimmer behind Angie's eyes, one that reminded Hannah of her own reckless party days, when she'd snuck around behind her parents' backs and avoided all discussion of "responsibilities."

"All right. Out with it." Hannah tried to imitate her mother's voice from back then.

Angie giggled and dropped her eyes back to her phone. "Can't a woman have her secrets?"

"Not in this house," Hannah said. "Besides, Mom. Look at me. I'm as big as a whale. If you're doing some kind of romantic living out there, you have to clue me in. Living vicariously is about the only way I'm going to live."

Angie pressed her lips together, her eyes scanning back and forth over the mysterious text message. Finally, she shrugged and said, mostly to the phone, "I met someone."

Hannah dropped her head back and screeched with excitement. Inside, it felt like her baby did a little backflip.

"Who is he? Or she! Sometimes, women decide they're totally done with men after divorce."

"Hannah…" Angie groaned.

"All right. He." Hannah gave her mother a sneaky smile. "I want every detail."

Angie sighed and positioned her phone in front of Hannah, where text messages from someone named Fletcher Baxter sat, waiting.

FLETCHER BAXTER: Hey there :)

FLETCHER BAXTER: Business brought me to Bar Harbor today.

FLETCHER BAXTER: I just finished and thought about you, my favorite pianist.

FLETCHER BAXTER: Any chance I could steal you away tonight?

Hannah blinked up at her mother, somewhere between shock and joy. "Mom. Who the heck is Fletcher Baxter?"

Angie's face broke into a wide grin. "Oh, he's that guy who's having the big party in August."

"The reason behind you putting together the band in the first place?" Hannah whispered.

"That's right."

"Wow. He must be really special," Hannah probed.

Angie nodded, her eyes widening. "My gut tells me he really is."

"You have to trust your gut in this life," Hannah told her simply. "It's all you have."

"I think you're correct in that."

Silence hung over them for a long moment. Hannah finally shrieked and said, "Mom! You have to write back. Don't leave him on 'Read'!"

"What does that even mean?" Angie cried. "You have to remember that I've hardly dated anyone before. I'm like a teenager."

"I don't know! Just, like, write him back? Tell him you're available?" Hannah shot back.

"But doesn't that make me seem too interested?" Angie demanded.

"That's BS," Hannah affirmed. "And besides. He used a smiley face, Mom. A smiley-face! That means he wants to kiss you on the mouth."

Angie burst into laughter all over again. "Is this how people talk these days?"

Hannah nodded so violently that her curls shook around her ears. "You better brush up on dating lingo."

Angie grabbed her phone back, furrowed her brow, and typed timidly. Her fingers tapped so slowly that Hannah yearned to grab the phone away from her and do it herself.

But as a new mother, she had to learn how to let people teach themselves.

After what seemed like a small infinity, Angie turned her phone around to show off what she'd written. It was short, simple, and, Hannah had to admit, almost perfect.

ANGIE: Welcome to Bar Harbor :)
ANGIE: I'd love to meet.
ANGIE: I'm available in about an hour.

Hannah nodded. "You're learning, Young Padawan."

Angie giggled. She placed her phone back on the table and strung her fingers through her hair, suddenly panicked. "Oh my God. Oh my God. I'm going on a date." She then jumped from the kitchen chair and fled into the bathroom, slamming the door behind her.

"Don't panic!" Hannah called.

But that, of course, was easier said than done.

About forty-five minutes later, a gorgeous woman stepped back into the kitchen— her hair styled, her waist cinched with a thick belt, her feet in sandals, and her perfume nuanced. Hannah wolf-whistled from her uncomfortable position on the corner chair, a large magazine spread out across her stomach.

"You're hot," she told her mother.

"Yeah. Right."

"Don't you dare undermine yourself," Hannah warned.

Angie groaned, adjusting the waistband of her black jeans and the top of her shirt. "Is it too booby?"

"Never," Hannah shot back, giving her a wink.

Angie sighed and took a dramatic step toward the door. "I feel like I'm headed to my doom."

"You're going to live," Hannah told her. "And if it totally sucks, I'll be right here."

"You'll be asleep in five minutes," Angie told her with assurance.

"That's true. But if you buy delicious snacks on your way home, I'll find a way to wake up."

Angie hovered over the kitchen table for a dramatic moment, eyeing the divorce papers. After a staggered breath, she hurriedly grabbed the blue pen and scribbled her name. She then let all the air out of her lungs and shrieked.

"Okay. Before I lose my nerve," she told Hannah. "I love you. So, so much."

She then disappeared into the gorgeous July night, leaving Hannah to hibernate alone.

Chapter Ten

It seemed miraculous that Fletcher Baxter waited precisely where he'd said he would. He looked like something out of a dream, stationed there on the harbor docks in a white t-shirt and a pair of dark jeans, his hands shoved in his pockets and the breeze off Frenchman Bay fluttering through his dark hair. Angie's heart literally skipped a beat, maybe two.

Wait. Did I just sign my divorce papers?

Did I actually take that leap?

"Hi," she heard herself say, praying it sounded cool and easy— not like a woman fresh in the dating pool.

"Hello, Ang." He said the nickname so easily, as though they'd known one another for years. He placed his hand on her shoulder and dropped his lips over her cheek, greeting her like a European in a film.

It was nearly eight. Although Angie hadn't eaten anything more than a few cheese-flavored chips from the dollar store, she'd lost all connection with her body and could hardly remember the concept of hunger. If Fletcher had suggested a seven-course meal, however, she'd have eaten it. She'd have done anything.

"I thought we might go for a sail," Fletcher said instead.

Angie's lips parted in surprise. Her eyes scanned across the frothing waves of Frenchman Bay, which eased out into the mighty Atlantic. Often, she thought about that wide expanse and the next patch of earth— miles and miles across nothingness.

"Unless sailing isn't your thing?" he asked.

In truth, Angie wasn't entirely sure it was. Luke had taken her out on his boat several afternoons, each time showing her the literal ropes and how to manipulate the sails. Each time, she'd felt her fear lessening. That didn't mean it would ever go away.

"The ocean is..." She trailed off, no longer capable of words.

"I think it's incorrect to ever lose fear of the ocean," Fletcher told her, cocking his head in that familiar way of his. "More than eighty percent of the ocean has never been explored by humans. We have no inkling of what goes on down there."

"You're not making it any easier for me to step out on that boat," Angie joked, her smile widening.

But here, Fletcher stretched out a strong hand, his eyes glittering. "Come on, Ang. Don't you trust me?"

Angie wasn't sure why she did. She felt herself lift one foot after another as she followed him closer and closer to the water's edge and then out onto the furthest dock, where Fletcher's friend's boat was tied up.

"He lets me take it out whenever I'm in the area," Fletcher explained. "We have a pretty long history of sailing together. There's a lot of trust there."

"He's here in Bar Harbor?" Angie asked.

"A bit outside," Fletcher explained. "He keeps to himself.

Kind of a hermit. Although, I can't say I blame him. As I get older, I find myself retreating more and more from human society. I watch the way people behave and the way people abuse their friends and family members and think to myself, do I really want to be involved in a world like this?"

Angie's heart lifted. Before she had time to respond, Fletcher stepped out onto the glossy shine of a sailboat, which dropped gently with his weight. Fletcher then turned and took her hand in his, guiding her to a safe position on the boat. Angie tried to explain that she knew a "thing or two" about sailing, but Fletcher seemed the sort of man who wanted to take charge, to take care of her. After seven months of having to care exclusively for herself and her daughter, Angie took a deep breath and allowed herself to fall into his nurturing ways.

It was a welcome change, one that Angie would remember for the rest of her life.

After only two fake dates at The Minty Green, Angie already felt as though she knew this man, the way he operated, the way he loved his family and upheld his friends. As they careened through the growing darkness, bucking over waves, they fell back into one of their textured conversations, discussing the intricacies of their lives.

For the first time, Fletcher expressed the fact that he'd been married before.

"It was a complete disaster," Fletcher said, smiling sadly. "I thought she was one type of person; she thought I was another. We were like two strangers, sleeping side-by-side."

Angie's throat tightened. "How long did it last?"

"Seven years," he told her, shaking his head in disbelief. "It makes me wonder what kind of man I was, staying in something that made me so miserable."

"Sometimes I wonder how many of my decisions were made for someone else's happiness," Angie breathed.

Fletcher's eyes glittered with recognition. "Sometimes, you

say things that make me see your soul so clearly. It feels like a soul I've known for much longer than just a week or two."

Angie dropped her eyes to her hands, which were wrapped foolishly over her knees. *Was this how you found your "soul mate"?* Had she ever considered her ex-husband to be her twin flame?

"I signed my divorce papers today." She spoke out across the inky ocean, eyes eastward toward Europe.

Fletcher held the silence for a long time. The only sound was the whipping winds and the splash of the waves.

Finally, he said, "You're brave, you know that?"

Angie blinked several times. "I don't feel brave. I feel like..." She thought for a moment, then gestured around her. "I feel like a boat without a harbor."

Fletcher laughed good-naturedly and dropped down to sit beside her, his hands still wrapped in ropes. He then draped his hand over her cheek and gazed into her eyes as he whispered, "You have a harbor. Right here, with me."

And after that, he leaned in and kissed her. Her eyes dropped closed, and she swam in impossible darkness as the boat rocked to-and-fro beneath her. When they came up for air, there was hardly anything for Angie to say except this:

"Please. Kiss me again."

Chapter Eleven

"If I hear you call yourself a whale again, I swear…" Abby warned Hannah dangerously, leaning toward her.

"You swear what?" Hannah shot back, her hand over her stomach as her lips twisted into a smile. "I'll have you know that tourists come to Maine from all over the world to check out our gorgeous population of passing whales. I'm a part of the tourism industry, Abby! And without the tourism industry, I ask you, could Bar Harbor truly stay alive?"

Abby grumbled inwardly and turned around, assessing something on her Canon camera. Hannah glanced to the other side of the outdoor reception area, watching as her mother and the rest of the jazz ensemble set up their chairs around a baby grand piano, which Natalie and Victor had rented purely for the sake of Angie's jazz ensemble. (Of this, Angie had simply shrugged and said, "I'll never understand people with money, but in this case, it's serving me well.") Hannah caught her mother's eye and gave her a silly wave, sticking out her tongue. Angie grinned back.

It was July 23rd, just an hour before Abby and Hannah's

official photograph duties were set to begin. The venue itself was, admittedly, far more beautiful than the website had advertised (this was something Abby had already suggested they reach out to the owners about for potential work). The main building was an old, ornate hotel built in the 1850s. The surrounding gardens and reception area echoed out from the main hotel before diminishing out to allow the rocks to line the coast. From where they stood, the sounds of waves rollicked over them, a constant reminder of the volatility of Maine's nature.

Abby and Hannah had arrived at the hotel early to investigate the afternoon light and finalize where, exactly, they wanted to position the couple for their photographs. Victor and Natalie had agreed to have their photographs taken prior to the service, which would allow a more seamless scheduling for all guests. "Nothing like waiting around for two or three hours for the bride and groom to show up to their own reception," Natalie had said sarcastically, "No way. We're not that kind of couple."

The reasoning behind this was linked to Natalie's need to be better than the competition. *The competition?* Other couples in her friendship group, of course. Abby and Hannah had had many laughs about this, unable to comprehend hating the people you were supposed to love so much.

Hannah set up her camera, maintaining an eye on her mother and her newly formed jazz band. That stoic drummer, Paul, was warming up on the drums, his arms and legs loose and his sticks thwapping with precision. The others, including Marvin, the saxophonist, Ashlee, the trumpeter, Hank, the bassist, and Megan, the trombonist, gathered around, puffing their cheeks around their mouth pieces or strumming the strings. Angie read something on a little notecard, probably the set list, as Hannah's heart seized with love.

It had been a long time since she'd seen her mother so focused. So happy.

"Hey, Han? We're about to do First Look," Abby said. "You ready?"

Hannah waddled over to the large oak tree, where they'd decided to feature the young couple's "First Look" photographs. According to wedding photography tradition, this "First Look" was meant to capture the same beauty of the groom seeing the bride for the first time as she walked down the aisle— without the annoyance of making your guests wait three hours for their dinner.

Hannah hated to admit it to herself, but she was both nervous and excited. This was their first big-time event, one that would hopefully prove Love Shack Photography worthy of other top-tier events— weddings, graduations, family reunions, engagements, vacations, and everything in between. Every moment seemed pivotal. Of this, Abby had joked that they just had to take a lot of photographs. "Some of them are bound to be good. We can figure that out in editing."

The groom, Victor, arrived at the scene of the "First Look" a few minutes early. To Hannah, he looked like a run-of-the-mill groom, with a traditional suit, shiny black shoes, and hair that looked a bit over-stylized, but in a way that would make him pop in the photographs. A thing that made him endearing, at least in Hannah's eyes, was his buggy-eyed, frightened look. He paced and shifted his weight, checking his expensive watch more times per minute than Hannah usually checked her phone per hour.

Hannah muttered how nervous he looked to Abby.

"I know," Abby breathed. "I guess if we do enough of these weddings, we'll have a script we can always use to calm people's nerves."

"Any ideas of one right now?" Hannah asked.

Abby shook her head. Just then, Victor's eyes scanned over to them, pausing for an overly long time on Hannah's stomach.

Of this, Hannah muttered, "See? I told you. The tourists come from miles around."

Abby scoffed. "He's just panicked. He sees you, and he knows this is what he's headed for."

"A big beer belly?" Hannah joked.

Abby rolled her eyes. "No, Han. Natalie obviously wants adorable little Brooklyn babies who wear little overalls and tiny hats."

"Right."

A few minutes after the set time, a bridesmaid came running to say that Natalie was just behind the door. "Victor needs to stand behind the tree."

Victor did as he was told, positioning himself with his arms behind his back and his chin lifted toward the eggshell blue of the sky. How quickly he moved reminded Hannah of a young boy, told to do his chores.

Natalie stepped from the shadows of the hotel, her cream-colored skirt lifted to avoid touching the ground. Her dress was vintage-inspired, puffy around her neck, with a large area cut out to feature her toned back. While Hannah did think the dress to be worthy of a magazine spread, it wasn't any fun in the slightest. It didn't seem romantic; it was Aristocratic, instead.

Abby instructed Natalie on where to stand, popping around easily. Hannah remained where she'd decided to stand for the "First Look." Together, she and Abby had decided that she'd remain more stationary throughout the first photography session, the walk down the aisle, and the reception itself, while Abby treated the affair like a photography marathon. "But it's perfect," Abby had explained, "because you can focus on the light and the angles, and I can just take a monstrous number of photographs."

Hannah knew that Abby didn't actually believe that— that

it would be better to have two photographers running around, taking surprise photographs, and featuring as many guests as they could. It just wasn't a possibility at this moment. Maybe someday.

When Victor did turn around for that official "First Look," Hannah lifted her camera and snapped as many photographs as she could, careful to capture every smile, every touch, every kiss. Throughout, she found it difficult to comprehend the weight of emotion between them. She was there to do a job, plain and simple.

That's why the next part of the afternoon struck her as terribly odd.

After an hour's worth of poses along the water and the gardens, Natalie and Victor bid one another goodbye with a "See you at the aisle!" and separated. Abby and Hannah followed behind Natalie, chatting about the day's events so far and whether or not Natalie had "eaten enough." According to several blogs that Abby and Hannah had read about weddings, many brides forgot to eat and ended up terribly drunk or terribly weak or both. Nobody wanted that.

"We'll just take some more shots of you and your bridesmaids," Abby suggested as they entered, greeting the twentysomething women, who all drank champagne and chatted easily. "You know. A few of just you girls, hanging out before the big moment."

Bridesmaid Candace greeted Abby and Hannah warmly, shrieking that she "absolutely adored" the new website and the "fresh but catchy" name for their business. She then bragged to the other bridesmaids about how she'd discovered Abby and Hannah spontaneously, describing their union the way one might describe having found ten dollars on the sidewalk. "I just stumbled into them!"

For the first fifteen minutes or so, Hannah and Abby operated as normal (if this was normal for a wedding?), taking photographs and chatting. Hannah grabbed probably more than her fair share of snacks before one of the bridesmaids shoved a cookie in her hand and said, "You need this way more than we do! I'm supposed to be able to stay in this dress all night long." She then leaned closer to whisper into Hannah's ear. "And oh my God, Natalie picked the tightest bridesmaids' outfits. Which you wouldn't have thought she would do since she's so, so jealous every time Victor looks at another girl."

Hannah's cheeks flashed pink with embarrassment. Still, she loved the honesty of this woman, someone she would never see again. "Does he do that a lot?"

The bridesmaid ignored her. Her eyes were glossy from champagne.

And suddenly, there was a crash, shattered glass, and a dramatic wail.

Hannah ducked around, still holding her half-eaten cookie. There, on the floor, surrounded by a growing stain of champagne and several shards of shattered glass, sat their bride. Natalie's cheeks were red and blotchy; tears had left streaks, taking with them black mascara and eyeliner down both cheeks. She looked like a woman on the verge of a breakdown.

"Oh, honey." The woman who'd given Hannah a cookie sounded almost gleeful.

"I just—" Natalie hiccupped. "I just don't know—" Another hiccup.

Abby and Hannah locked eyes across the room. Abby removed her camera from her neck and stepped toward the bride tentatively. Two of the bridesmaids helped Natalie to her feet and placed her on a chair. Abby began to collect the shards of glass with delicate fingers, placing them in a big plastic bag that had once held what looked to be a sandwich.

"Honey, what is it?" a bridesmaid demanded.

"I don't know!" Natalie cried.

"Oh, God." Another bridesmaid coughed. "Is it Tommy? Do you miss him?"

Natalie's eyes welled with tears. Again, Abby and Hannah locked eyes. *Was Tommy an ex? What?* Had Hannah not been hanging on this wedding for its monetary worth, she would have lapped this up as good gossip. As it stood, she still hadn't been paid.

"It's not Tommy." Natalie hiccupped again. "I just. Gosh. I look at Victor and I..."

"What, honey?" The bridesmaids were getting impatient. Nobody wanted to wear those tight dresses for much longer, that was sure. But it was far better to get this show on the road than wait another three or four years for Natalie to meet Mr. Right Number Two, get engaged, and pick out another, equally as uncomfortable dress.

"I just love him so much!" Natalie cried. "I love him so much. But what about after today? What happens next? What if he falls out of love with me? What if I fall out of love with him? What if he has an affair with his secretary, and I'm mortified? What if he gets hit by the F-Train?"

Each of Natalie's fears grew louder, more frantic. She swiped her hand over her cheeks, smearing her black makeup even more.

Before she knew what she'd done, Hannah stepped out of the room and into the splendor of the sun. She waddled toward the pianist at the baby grand, who spoke in soft tones to the trumpeter, Ashlee while pointing to something on a sheet of music. When Hannah got close enough, Angie's eyes lifted to find her. Her smile was twisted with worry.

"What is it?"

Hannah led Angie back to the hiccupping bride. As Angie sat across from her, the other bridesmaids gave her a wide berth, sensing her wisdom and strength. Angie took Natalie's hand in hers and gave her the news that, ultimately, she had to hear.

"Honey, as humans, we can never know what will happen next."

Natalie hiccupped in answer. Her eyes were stony. "That's why I'm so upset."

Angie nodded. "I know. I know that." She swallowed. "But what's the conclusion of all this sorrow? Do you want to go out there and tell Victor the marriage is off, all because you're worried he'll get run over by a train someday?"

From someone else's lips, the idea seemed both heinous and funny at once. Natalie wrinkled her nose and snorted into laughter. "I'm so dumb," she breathed.

"You're no dumber than the rest of us," Angie told her, cupping one of her hands with both of hers. "But I will tell you this." Her eyes flashed toward Hannah's. "I am divorced. My husband hurt me very, very badly after more than two decades of marriage. But you know what?"

Natalie, frowning, shook her head almost imperceptibly.

"I would do it all over again in a heartbeat," Angie told her simply. "The good times far outweigh the bad. I loved him with my whole heart and soul and mind for a very long time. There's no getting that time back, that's true. But damn, am I glad I did it."

Chapter Twelve

"That was a close one," Hannah muttered to Angie as they followed the bride and groom away from one-hundred and fifty white-painted wooden chairs. The surrounding crowd hollered and cried their congratulations as "This Will Be Our Year" wailed from the speakers. The bride and groom linked hands and raced away from their guests as Abby chased after them, taking as many photographs as she could.

"I think they're going to be all right," Angie said under her breath.

"What makes you say that?"

Angie shrugged. "It's just a feeling." She allowed a beat to pass before she added, "It was a beautiful ceremony, though. It felt strangely real. Less hokey than I thought it would."

Hannah nodded. "I think I know what you mean."

Angie stepped forward and fell in line with Paul, the drummer. Paul nodded firmly and lifted his drumsticks from his pocket. "I guess it's showtime for us?"

"That's right," she said, a smile sneaking toward her ear. She turned to kiss Hannah on the cheek and wished her luck for the night ahead. It would be a long one.

Angie sat at the edge of her piano bench, watching as her newly formed band sat, adjusting their stands and preparing their music. Only Paul had no music. When she'd asked him how on earth he expected to perform that evening, he'd told her that he'd memorized all of their planned pieces. This, to Angie, was insanity. She'd tried not to let on how impressed she was.

Across the gardens, the wedding guests sat at round tables with white tablecloths, sipping champagne and chatting about the ceremony, complimenting one another's outfits, and inquiring about the dinner ahead. Angie made eye contact with each of the members of her jazz band, then gave Paul his cue. As he was the drummer, it was up to him to set up each song.

They began— first with "I've Got You Under My Skin," a jazz classic that, in Angie's opinion, had a bite to it. Already, the mood across the reception shifted; laughter rang out more joyously; people turned their heads to listen. Live music allowed reality to transcend into something else. Angie had always believed in that.

Over the next two and a half hours, Angie and her brand-new jazz ensemble played their prepared pieces, transitioning easily from one track to the next. Although they'd practiced together no more than three times, Angie felt a certainty about their performance. They simply "gelled." Frequently throughout the performance, she and Paul locked eyes— only for a split second— just to check-in. Paul's eyes remained half-open and his motions easy. Angie wasn't sure how she knew he was pleased with the performance. It was just a gut feeling, like everything else. How could she trust it?

When the guests finished their meal, and the cake was officially cut, the bride approached Angie to tell her that the DJ was just about ready to take over for the night. Natalie gushed, her eyes welling with tears as she told Angie she "hadn't fully known what to expect" when she'd hired Angie's jazz band. "But you're spectacular. You really are." She then paused, her hand still on Angie's wrist. "Thank you again for everything you said. When I saw Victor as I came down the aisle, I felt like I could see all of it. Every single beautiful year that we'll spend." She blinked back tears. "I can't believe I almost gave all that away."

After the band was cleared for the night, one of the caterers showed them to a separate table, just for them, and served them their meal. Angie had selected salmon, perfectly seasoned, with plenty of lemon drizzled on top. Paul, seated beside her, had opted for the vegan option— something that looked mostly potato-based and pretty bad. Paul squashed it with his fork.

"Are you vegan?" Angie asked.

Paul shook his head. "No. I just get nervous about catering events. I picture all that food beneath a heater, taking on diseases."

Angie laughed and took another bite of her salmon. "Are you sure you don't want part of my fish?"

Paul eyed her salmon longingly.

"Come on," she coaxed. "I won't be able to eat all of it."

This, of course, was a lie. But she was so terribly pleased with both Paul and the rest of her jazz ensemble. She couldn't possibly let her drummer go hungry.

Paul took a bite and then a second one, but soon stopped and focused on his wine. Around the table, other members of the jazz ensemble joked and laughed together, falling into friendship easily. Angie gave Paul a sidelong glance. *Why was he at such a distance from the rest of the world? What was going on in that head of his?*

"Have you played in other wedding ensembles?" she asked.

Paul looked uncomfortable with the question. "A few times."

"Gotcha." Angie forced a smile. It felt unnatural. "Did you get food poisoning at those?"

Paul shook his head and began to mash his potatoes again. Angie cursed herself for acting "strange." Her fingers fluttered over the tablecloth, collected her wine glass, and tossed the contents down her throat. By the time the caterer had arrived to refill her glass for the third time, she'd gotten it into her head that she wanted— no, needed— to text Fletcher.

God, she'd had a marvelous time with him the other evening. He was intelligent and kind and thoughtful. He remembered things about her, intimate things she'd told him about the heaviness of her life. They'd kissed for what had felt like an hour, folding their bodies into each other. When he'd dropped her off later that night, she'd floated up the stairs to her apartment and fallen back in bed, her heart pounding.

This, her gut told her, was true love.

Now, what to text him? According to Hannah, the rules of texting were always: keep it simple. Nobody wanted to read a book of your thoughts, no matter how much they thought they liked you. "I've seen relationships die on a boring, long text," Hannah had explained. The idea had terrified Angie.

ANGIE: I had a really nice time the other night.

Now that was simple.

Angie blinked down at it, feeling slightly woozy but not overly drunk. She definitely hadn't been too drunk to text him. *Right?* She lifted her eyes to try to find Hannah, the only woman she knew "in the know." But Hannah was hard at work, waddling around with her camera lifted, capturing what she could of the reception.

Suddenly, something wonderful happened.

The two checkmarks beneath Angie's text message suddenly turned blue. According to Hannah, this meant that the recipient had read the messages. Angie's heart began to pump. Obviously, this meant that Fletcher was about to write her back. He'd been waiting for her to say something, anything. Now, she'd started a fresh line of communication.

It was time to fall in love again.

But in the full two minutes that followed, as Angie stared down at the text message, nothing happened. Her heart thudded as her anxiety grew.

Someone said her name. Angie lifted her eyes to find the bassist, Hank, sliding into the chair beside her, asking some questions about her musical background back in Chicago. Did she know this-or-this person? Did she ever go to this-or-this restaurant? She hardly heard what he said but felt herself nodding along, engaging. Occasionally, she glanced over at Paul, who seemed in a world all his own. Did he feel as alone as he looked? Probably that wasn't a question she could ask him. Loneliness wasn't a thing you talked about.

She checked her phone again. Still no answer. A caterer approached to refill her glass, which she accepted gladly, no longer questioning the concept of more wine, more wine. "Yes, please, more wine."

An hour passed, then another. Occasionally, Hannah collapsed in whatever chair was nearest Angie at the time, depending on who in her jazz ensemble had either left or gotten another slice of cake or hit the dance floor. Hannah looked happy, her cheeks crimson and her legs quivering from the weight of her pregnant body. She took photographs of her mother, asking that she at least try to smile. Angie didn't have the strength to tell Hannah that her heart was breaking all over again. She'd been stupid enough to put her trust in someone who shouldn't have mattered at all.

"Are you having a good time, Mom?" Hannah asked softly across the table. It was a little before midnight, and no text message had come through.

"I feel right as rain," Angie lied, forcing a smile. "We did it, honey."

"It's not such a bad start, is it?" Angie whispered, the tears in her eyes catching the light.

"Not in the least," Angie breathed. "Our hard work is paying off. Now, we just have to keep going."

Chapter Thirteen

"I've never seen so much cash."

Monday morning, Hannah and Abby stood in front of four thousand dollars in cash, which lined a small black suitcase. It looked as though they'd been involved in some kind of drug deal. Hannah's fingers fluttered over the green paper, taking stock of the hundreds and fifties.

"Natalie said her dad always pays in cash," Abby said with a shrug. "Apparently, he thinks it's cleaner that way."

"I'm just glad we got it back to the Keating Inn," Hannah breathed, lifting her eyes to the safe, where they'd stored the cash the previous two days.

"Me too." Abby wiped a tear from her cheek and eyed the clock on the wall. "The bank downtown just opened. You should be good to go."

A shiver raced up and down Hannah's spine. As they'd driven back to downtown Bar Harbor Saturday night, Hannah and Abby had discussed business options and appropriate strategies, parroting advice they'd gotten from small business websites and blogs. Ultimately, they'd decided that they needed to open up a business account for Love Shack Photography. Immediately.

"Oh," Abby began. "I almost forgot. Yesterday, we got another three requests for work. An engagement session, a wedding, and a graduation photo session— all in the next two months."

Hannah puffed out her cheeks. "Good thing we're opening this business account, then."

"You sure you're good to do this on your own?" Abby asked.

Hannah nodded, although she obviously felt complicated about it. What the heck did she know about opening a business account? Abby passed over the paperwork she'd filled out about her own personal part of the company, along with her passport and driver's license, both necessary for opening the account. Hannah's were already in her purse.

Abby winced as she returned the bookshelf to its rightful place over the safe. She then wiped her palms over her thighs and led Hannah and the suitcase back behind the front desk, where two guests from Saturday's wedding were waiting, ready to check out. Abby and Hannah greeted them warmly.

"There he is," Hannah teased the man. "Last I saw you, you were shot-gunning a beer way too close to the bride and her fancy dress."

The man blushed knowingly, glancing at his wife, fearful of retribution. The wife groaned and said, "Every time he gets drunk, he always challenges people to shot-gun beers."

The man puffed out his chest like a frat boy, proud of what he stood for and all he was. "I can't help that I'm the best at it," he explained. His wife rolled her eyes.

After the couple disappeared, packed up their car, and fled Bar Harbor forever, Hannah and Abby hugged goodbye. Abby groaned, "Please, don't leave me here at the front desk to die."

To this, Hannah affirmed, "If we keep going like we're going? You'll be out of here in no time."

Abby followed Hannah to the front porch of the Keating Inn, where they stood chatting for another few minutes. They watched from a distance as the construction crew continued to build up the brand-new Keating House, further back in the Keating Property, discussing Casey and Grant and the fact that, only just last December, they'd almost divorced. Hannah thought their reunion was genuinely incredible.

"It's wild that people can be forgiven and move forward," Hannah breathed. After a long moment of reflection, she added, "Although I have to admit. I'm a model for that, too. I know you ate the donut I was saving in the Keating Inn refrigerator."

Abby's jaw dropped open. "I did not!"

"You did." Hannah heaved a sigh. "But like I said. I'm learning to live with it. And I think our business might even survive."

"Oh my God." Abby rolled her eyes into the back of her head. "It was probably one of the ten other people who work here!"

"La la la. I can't hear you!" Hannah buried the suitcase beneath her arm and waddled down the front steps of the gorgeous Keating Inn, headed for the car that she and her mother shared. Once inside, she honked the horn and watched as Abby flailed an arm with excitement. Hannah's heart swelled with gladness. She could never have imagined any of this.

Hannah parked on the street directly alongside the Bar Harbor Bank, took a deep breath, then heaved her rotund form out of the car. She then grabbed the suitcase and waddled into the branch, which bustled with life. The reason, she supposed, was that Bar Harbor was still something of an old-fashioned town. People liked to deal with their bank tellers directly rather than over the phone or online. There was a sweetness to this, she supposed.

Hannah joined a line of three and waited, shifting her weight from foot to foot. At the front of the line, a woman spoke to the teller about re-mortgaging her house, a thought that terrified Hannah. There were so many "real life" things that petrified her. First, she had to deal with setting up a business bank account. Next? Labor and delivery. After that? God, she didn't even want to think about that. Not yet. *One thing at a time, Hannah. One thing at a time.*

By the time it was Hannah's turn, a line of six people stood behind her, chatting excitedly, awash with gladness that Monday morning. Hannah had never known the bank to be a place for social outings.

"Can I help you?" The teller was in her late forties, perhaps, with thick red bangs and a pin that said, "Bar Harbor Aquatics."

Hannah placed the suitcase on the counter between them and whispered, "I need to set up a business account."

The woman couldn't hear her. "What did you say, honey?"

"A business account," Hannah said. "I need help setting up a business account!"

The woman closed her eyes knowingly, grabbed a pad of paper and a stack of folders, and gestured for Hannah to follow her. When they met on the far end of the counter, the woman staggered back with surprise, her eyes on Hannah's stomach.

"I had no idea you were..." The bank teller shook her head, sensing she was in gray territory. "I just. From above. You don't look..."

Hannah groaned inwardly and continued to waddle toward the side room. "Don't worry about it," she told the woman. "If I had it my way, this pregnancy would be over immediately. But it's only July 25th. I've got about a month left to go."

Once inside the private office, the bank teller, who, by

now, had introduced herself as Sharon, cinched the blinds closed between the office and the rest of the bank. Hannah collapsed on the cushioned chair on one side of the desk while Sharon knelt herself gently upon the one on the other. Hannah then unlatched the suitcase with the secret code to display the four thousand. The woman nodded, unimpressed. *Obviously, if you worked at a bank, money wasn't impressive to you anymore.*

Sharon began to explain the specifics of setting up a business account. Hannah only half-listened, her brain going into a weird slump she called "baby brain." Sharon began to type out both Abby and Hannah's information on the desk computer, asking various questions like the nature of the business along with the name. When Hannah confessed to "Love Shack Photography," Sharon stopped dead and eyed her with surprise. "I just love that song," she said, her excitement growing. "It's a perfect name."

Yet again, Hannah gave her mother a private thanks. *How had she known?*

Sharon continued to outline relevant tax information and the process of how Abby and Hannah would "pay themselves out" per month, should they want to. Hannah laughed at that, saying that, absolutely, they would eventually want that. She tapped her stomach lovingly as Sharon laughed.

"I have two of my own," Sharon told her knowingly. "But I had them a bit later in life. Thirty-five and thirty-seven."

Hannah's eyes widened with surprise. It was a rare thing, especially in the Bar Harbor area, to hear about older moms. This personal story endeared Hannah to Sharon all the more. Everyone across the great and varied earth had some sort of story.

But about ten seconds later, everything in Hannah, Sharon, and everyone else at Bar Harbor Bank's lives changed forever.

There was a sudden cry of alarm, followed by a crash.

Then came a terrible smack of metal on metal. A masculine voice cried, "GET ON THE GROUND."

Hannah and Sharon's eyes locked. The suitcase remained between them, wide open. Sharon closed it quickly and hid it behind the desk before whispering, "Get on the ground. Cooperate with everything they say."

Hannah had never been more petrified in her life.

Bit by bit, she dropped herself to the ground, placing her hand over her pregnant belly and staring at the ceiling. Tears welled in her eyes and drifted down her cheeks, dampening her hair. When she'd been a child, sometimes, Angie had been too overwhelmed with love and fear— crying into Hannah's hair as she'd held her at night. That was back when Hannah had learned, firsthand, that her mother felt everything at a higher pitcher than most people. It was, in fact, a superpower.

God, all she could think about was her mother.

Her mother and her unborn baby.

A baby she could hardly picture, as she'd never learned its sex.

They say that time moves slower when you're panicked, that you can fully experience every single aching thought. Throughout the following grueling minutes, Hannah's ears were perked, listening as the men threatened each and every person within the bank.

"If you move, we'll blow your brains out," one of the robbers said.

"You better stay on the floor, old man," another cried.

If Hannah had to guess, there were two, maybe three robbers within the bank. One of them currently spoke to a bank teller, who hadn't been able to stop crying since they'd entered. He threatened her, telling her that if she couldn't find a way to stop crying, he'd shoot her in the leg. This made her scream-cry all the more.

Had Hannah been in a better mood and in a different environment, she would have called the robber an idiot. You couldn't exactly get what you want out of someone by telling them to stop feeling what they were feeling. That was just first-grade logic.

Throughout, Hannah prayed and prayed that the men wouldn't open the door to the side office. For a little while, she thought that God had answered her prayers.

Unfortunately, one of the robbers kicked the door open and howled, "Now, what do we have in here?"

And that was when Hannah officially revealed herself to the robbers as "someone they hadn't planned for."

"Oh no. Oh no." The robber who'd kicked the door began to stagger back.

"What's gotten into you?" Another of the robbers bucked toward him, flashing his gun.

The first pointed down at Hannah, who, yes, was just about as big as a whale in pregnancy terms. Hannah wanted to chastise them for fat-shaming, but she was far too petrified for something like that.

"I don't know. I don't know about this," the first robber began, muttering to himself.

"Come on! Whatever!" Another bank robber bolted toward them, still turning his gun around the place to make sure everyone was accounted for. "So what. She's pregnant. This other lady's old as dirt. This guy over here might have a heart attack any second. Remember what we said. No risk, no reward."

The other two bank robbers locked eyes, having some kind of monstrous conversation through the air. Hannah's tongue turned to sandpaper.

"We need you two to come in here," the more confident bank robber told Hannah and Sharon. "Now!"

Hannah fidgeted there on the ground. Her brain told her body to move her over to the main foyer, to toil on the floor alongside the other victims. *But honestly? Who was she kidding?* When was the last time she'd managed to get up off the ground on her own?

Sharon raised her hand knowingly. The bank robbers didn't notice for a few seconds before blaring out, "What?" They also called her something horrible, a word that Sharon truly didn't deserve.

"I really am sorry to interrupt, sirs. But I don't believe she'll be able to move," Sharon explained.

The bank robbers were irritated beyond belief. They muttered under their breaths about what to do before one of them bucked forward and instructed Sharon to help him move Hannah into the next room. Hannah imagined herself calling a friend back in Chicago and explaining the events of this day. *A bank robber had to help my pregnant butt up off the ground. Can you believe it?*

Together, Sharon and the bank robber heaved Hannah up. All the blood dropped from Hannah's head and raced down her legs. Hannah then hobbled into the main room, where she found twelve people, two bank tellers and ten Bar Harbor residents, in the greatest fear of their lives. Slowly, Hannah eased herself down the wall and positioned her legs out in front of her, eyeing the bank robber with pleading eyes. This was all she could manage for him.

Don't hurt me. Don't hurt my baby.

Her heart hammered with longing.

This is all I ask of you.

Please.

Chapter Fourteen

Several blocks away from the Bar Harbor Bank, Angie and her jazz ensemble met for a three-hour rehearsal. To prepare, they warmed up separately— Angie fluttering her fingers across the keys, Ashlee blowing steam through her trumpet, Paul took control of his drum set, his eyes half-open. Within that downtown practice room, the sound was immense, a physical being that seemed to press against the walls and threaten to blast them to the ground.

As their warmup petered out, Angie chuckled to herself and eyed each of the members of her band. "For just a little ensemble, we manage to create a whole wall of sound."

Ashlee laughed, adjusting herself on the chair next to Marvin, the saxophonist. The air stiffened strangely, as though nobody knew quite how to feel in the silence. Perhaps that's why they'd all gotten into music— as a way to fight the silence.

"I wanted to thank you all for Saturday's performance," Angie added, squeezing her hands together anxiously. "We got so many compliments from wedding guests. A few people left business cards on my piano, telling me that they need music for their business socials or family reunions." Angie's smile broke wider. "So, prepare yourselves for a busy late summer and autumn, I suppose."

Paul rolled his drumsticks over the cymbals as the others clapped their hands joyously. It almost felt like they got away with something. People were willing to pay them to do what they loved to do the most.

"Okay. Okay. Compliment session over," Angie said. "Now, it's time for the hard part."

Marvin groaned, laughing. "Uh oh. She's about to crack the whip, guys."

"That's right," Angie returned with a sneaky smile. "I've been told I'm a perfectionist, for better or for worse. There were multiple sections that didn't quite meet my standards."

At his drum set, Paul nodded knowingly, as though he'd been right there with her, sensing the same troubling moments. This warmed Angie's heart.

"But after we finish fine-tuning those sections, I'd like to focus on improvisation," Angie continued. "As far as I'm concerned, if we can't improv together, we're not really a jazz ensemble. We're more like a boring band that imitates past jazz bands. To me, that's a boring fate."

Angie instructed the players to flip through their sheet music to page six of "My Funny Valentine," where a chord change and a tempo shift had left them staggering during Saturday's performance. Bit-by-bit, they worked through the measures— first slowly, then faster and faster. Angie was pleased with the ease with which her jazz ensemble took direction. Occasionally, Paul even interjected, saying he still felt a strange syncopation and insisting they go back to do it again.

At forty-five minutes past their start-time, Angie allowed her ensemble a few minutes for water and conversation. She leafed into her purse to check her phone, curious about whether or not Hannah had made it to the bank that morning.

To her surprise, there was no message from Hannah— just a barrage of answers from Fletcher Baxter himself. Finally.

FLETCHER BAXTER: Hi, Angie. I just received your messages.

FLETCHER BAXTER: I have to apologize. I was away most of the weekend due to family matters.

FLETCHER BAXTER: I had such a wonderful time with you. I haven't been able to get you out of my mind since.

FLETCHER BAXTER: I'll see you soon, I hope? And I hope we're still on for my party. Your jazz ensemble is an essential part. :)

Angie's eyes fluttered closed. She pressed the phone against her chest, her shoulders falling back. *Was this what "swooning" was?* Around her, the jazz ensemble continued to banter and laugh, showing off funny scales on their instruments and asking one another about their musical pasts.

She should have known better not to panic. What she and Fletcher had was obviously real. He'd explained himself; that's all that mattered.

"What's gotten into you?" Ashlee asked as she walked past the piano, bottle of water in hand.

Angie grimaced and rolled her eyes.

"Uh oh," Ashlee said, pointing her finger knowingly. "You've got that woozy teenage lovey-dovey look in your eye."

"Oh, I do not." Angie laughed and pushed her phone back into her purse once more. She eyed the clock on the wall, preparing to reel her jazz members back in for another forty-five minutes of rehearsal.

Before she could, however, there was a sudden knock on the door. Angie eyed where the sound had come from, annoyed. Who in their right mind would interrupt their rehearsal? She couldn't stand for it. She waved a hand to her co-musicians and said, "I'm sure it's nothing. Let's get started again." But a split-second later, the knock rang out with even more insistence. There was no ignoring it.

"Excuse me," Angie said, standing and stomping to the door. She then heaved a sigh and opened the door to discover, to her immense surprise, her little brother, Luke.

"Luke! What are you doing here?" All the blood drained from her head and dropped to her feet. Immediately, she thought the worst (or at least, what she thought was "the worst" right then). "Is Mom okay?"

"Angie, you need to come with me immediately."

Angie shifted her weight. "Luke, please. Just tell me what's going on." Fear didn't allow her to lower her voice. All her co-musicians could hear exactly what was going on.

Luke spread his fingers through his hair. There was the sound of a crash behind her. Angie turned as Paul leaped up from his drum set, stabbing his drumsticks into his pocket.

"It's Hannah," Luke finally told her, his voice cracking.

"What?" Angie shook her head, remembering the date on the calendar: AUGUST 22. "She's early. It's too early."

But Luke waved his hands. "It's not the baby."

Angie's heart dropped into her stomach.

"There's an incident at the bank," Luke continued. "I was at the Keating Inn when I heard about it. Abby freaked, saying that Hannah had just gone there to open a business account. She started calling her and calling her, but she's not answering the phone."

Suddenly, Paul was beside Angie, his hand on her shoulder to stabilize her. She wavered, her tongue swelling in her mouth.

"I don't understand. An incident at the bank?" Angie's voice no longer belonged to her.

"Men have locked off the bank," Luke continued to explain, at a loss. "They're keeping everyone inside hostage until they get what they want. Presumably money."

"We have to go." This was Paul, sounding urgent. Angie blinked up into his chocolate brown eyes with confusion. "Come on, Angie. Time is of the essence right now."

Angie grabbed her purse and slung it over her shoulder. With abstract thoughts, she considered what she had in her wallet. Twenty dollars, tops. She had nothing to negotiate with. What was she going to do?

She tried to make sense of the situation, but she just couldn't. She felt like she was living somebody else's life.

As Paul, Luke, and Angie hustled toward the bank, the other members of the jazz ensemble were hot on their heels. Already, it seemed, they cared for Angie and counted her as a future friend and confidant. There was no way they would let her go through this pain alone.

Even a full block back, it was clear that a massive crowd had gathered around the Bar Harbor Bank. Angie, Paul, and Luke barrelled through that crowd, forcing themselves to the front. Just like in the movies, the Bar Harbor police force had created a perimeter around the bank, ensuring that bystanders were far enough away from the front door and windows.

Brittany Keating's boyfriend, Brad, was a Bar Harbor police officer. Angie had worked with him diligently in the spring to take down Brittany's ex-husband in the wake of Brittany's robbery. Now, Angie flailed an arm to flag down Brad, whose face looked fatigued and wrinkled like wet paper.

By the time Brad reached Angie, Angie shuddered with fear and rage. She was too terrified to cry.

"Brad, my daughter's in there," Angie rasped, grabbing his arm right beneath his police patch. "My baby. She's pregnant. She's in her last term and ready to give birth at any moment."

Brad's eyes were glassy. "We're in the process of getting a phone into the bank to communicate with the perpetrators."

Angie stuttered with disbelief. "And what happens then?"

"We need to communicate with the robbers at all times," Officer Brad explained. "Figure out what they want and how we can get the hostages out safely."

Beside Angie, Paul stiffened. She blinked up at him, still confused why he'd stuck by her side like this. One of the cops called Officer Brad back over, and Brad nodded to Angie, explaining, "I have to get back. We're doing everything we can." After a beat, he added, "And please, Angie. Maintain the perimeter. It's essential for your safety."

Angie wanted to break something. How dare this man tell her what was "essential to her safety"? Her daughter was in there, taken hostage. Hannah was at the mercy of men with guns.

It was insanity.

Suddenly, Paul turned to face her. His chocolate eyes were her only anchor to the real world.

"Angie? I'll take care of this." He let a beat pass before he added, "You have to trust me."

And with that, Paul ducked under the yellow police tape and marched with purpose directly toward Officer Brad. Angie's heart seized with fear. *What on earth did the mysterious drummer of her band have to do with this?* Angie's hands fell to her sides, utterly helpless.

Suddenly, Marvin took the place of Paul, muttering, "Where is Paul going?"

Angie shook her head, at a loss. "He said he'd take care of it."

"What the heck does he know about something like this?"

But before them, Paul and Officer Brad were already deep in conversation. Officer Brad's eyebrows furrowed like big caterpillars over his eyes. He seemed to take stock in whatever it was Paul told him.

And suddenly, Officer Brad gestured toward another officer, who grabbed what looked like a bulletproof vest from the back of a police van. With an easy motion, Paul wrapped the bulletproof vest around his sturdy frame, placed a helmet on his head, and gave Officer Brad a firm nod.

What the heck was going on?

As he marched toward the bank, the drumsticks poked out from his pocket, pointing toward the gray summer sky.

Chapter Fifteen

The pain began about thirty minutes after the hostage situation began.

At first, the cramps were a dull discomfort at the base of Hannah's spine. Minutes later, they wrapped around to the front, carving into her the way her menstrual cramps once had. Dread pounded in her heart as the wave of pain crashed over her before receding once more.

When it was finished, she was coated in sweat and gasping for air. This, she knew, was not normal. This, she knew, was something far more than false labor. But it wasn't exactly perfect timing.

All the while, the bank robbers kept their guns at their sides and spoke in whispers. One of them was in conversation with the bank teller behind the counter, who struggled to speak between crying sessions.

"You need to focus up," the bank robber told her forcefully. "And tell me how much money is on site."

It was clear that the robbery wasn't going as planned. Although Hannah had never staged a robbery, she had to imagine that the initial planning stage probably felt a whole lot different than the real thing. The minute you found yourself waving a gun at a pregnant woman, for example, you probably re-evaluated and wondered how the heck you'd gotten here.

Although Hannah couldn't see outside the blinds on the bank windows, she guessed that already, the Bar Harbor Police Force had gathered outside. Probably, gossip had traveled quickly across town. Where was Angie in all of this? Hannah remembered what she'd written on the calendar— a three-hour rehearsal with her jazz band, all before lunchtime. Hannah had called her mother "obsessed." She'd then wrapped her arms around Angie and held her, whispering how proud she was of her. Angie had glowed.

Most of Hannah hoped that Angie hadn't yet learned about the hostage situation. She wanted to picture her behind the piano, eyes half-closed as she sculpted a gorgeous performance. She didn't want her mother to live in fear.

Another violent pain wrapped around Hannah's abdomen. She winced, closing her eyes. Whatever this was, she didn't want the bank robbers to notice. When they neared her, they brought their guns. She wanted them as far away from her as possible.

"What do you mean?" The bank robber howled this to the bank teller behind the counter, clearly enraged. "That's all the money you have on-site?" He turned his head quickly to gaze at the other bank robbers, whose shoulders slumped. "Well, that's not good enough for us. Is it, boys?"

The other two bank robbers seemed to consider this. Hannah wondered how much money the men were after. *What did they need to pay for? Medical bills? Legal bills? What?* Hannah marveled at the wage disparity in the country, about the horrific decisions people felt they had to make to stay afloat. She and Abby had been "lucky" enough to start their own business, something that Hannah prayed would eventually pay all her bills. (That said, Hannah had then been unlucky enough to be involved in a hostage situation. *You win some, you lose some.*)

Again, pain. A strange animal noise escaped Hannah's lips, one that caught the attention of Sharon, who lay on the floor closest to Hannah.

Before Hannah could stop her, Sharon howled out. "Oh my God. Do you realize that this poor woman is in labor?"

Probably, Sharon saw this as an opportunity to free all of them. But Hannah saw this only as positioning Hannah and her unborn child against the dangerous bank robbers. Her eyes popped open with rage as she stared Sharon down. She'd never hated anyone more.

But almost immediately, the pain returned, sharper this time. Hannah cried out, louder than ever. Now that everyone knew, she could belt out her feelings.

The bank robber behind the counter muttered several expletives. The other two, nearer to Hannah, looked down at her with big eyes. They looked like cartoon characters, with their black ski masks and their buggy eyes.

"You need to let us out!" one of the hostages chose this opportunity to cry out. "She's in labor! Do you want to put an unborn baby in danger? Is that what you really want to do?"

"Shut up!" the bank robber behind the counter howled, flashing his gun. He sounded terribly frightened.

"But he's right, man. We have to do something," another bank robber stammered.

"I don't know how to deliver a baby. Do you?" the other demanded.

Hannah closed her eyes and allowed the pain to flow through her. She'd read somewhere about not fighting it. *Had that been on a Mommy Blog? Had she actually begun to read Mommy Blogs? God, who was she?* One minute, she'd been a hot music student at the University of Chicago. The next, she was a washed-up pregnant hostage.

Life comes at you fast.

The next few minutes passed in a flurry of pain. The bank robbers passed around a lot of violent words, both to one another and the other hostages. They hadn't spoken to Hannah yet; they probably viewed her as a kind of bomb.

Suddenly, there was a loud knock at the door. One of the bank robbers howled. "This was a mistake!"

But another peeked through the blinds of the bank and said, "They've got us surrounded."

"Haven't you idiots seen the movies?" the last robber demanded. He, too, peeked through the blinds. "They've left a phone on the mat. They want to talk to us."

"We can't talk to the cops!"

"How the hell else do you think we'll get out of here?"

The robbers fought for another full minute. The pain in Hannah's abdomen and back roared so loudly that she found it difficult to focus on what they said. Finally, with a disgruntled howl, one of the bank robbers opened the door just the slightest bit, making sure to keep his gun in full view. He then grabbed the phone and slammed the door again.

With a shivering hand, he lifted the phone to his ear. The other gun flashed sharply at his side.

"Hello," he grunted into the phone. "We have a situation in here." He swallowed, turning his buggy eyes toward Hannah, sweating on the floor. "One of our hostages just went into labor. We need to get her out of her, pronto."

Chapter Sixteen

"**A**ngie! Angie! Hey! That's my sister-in-law. Move aside."

Heather's voice rang out over the chaos of the crowd. Angie turned to find those ocean blue eyes, staring her down as Heather looked through the throngs of people. A split second later, Heather's arms were around Angie as Angie pressed her forehead onto Heather's shoulder. She shivered against her, hearing only the violent beating of her heart and Heather's whispered, "It's going to be okay. It's going to be okay."

The logical voice in the back of Angie's head told her that Heather really had no idea if anything would work itself out. Still, it was something you had to say in times of crisis, a reason to move forward.

Over Angie's head, Heather and Luke spoke in soft tones. Luke updated her with what he knew thus far, that the drummer in Angie's band had been suited up in a bulletproof vest and now seemed in steady conversation with the rest of the officers.

"Is that Brad?" Heather asked.

"Yep. Have you seen Brittany around?"

"God, no. I guess she already knows about this, though. The whole town does. She has to know that Brad's doing all he can to get them out," Heather whispered.

"The officers just dropped what looked like a phone or a walkie-talkie in front of the door of the bank," Luke explained. "One of them opened the door to retrieve it, showing his gun the entire time."

"No!" Heather sounded petrified.

"It was really intense," Luke admitted.

Angie lifted her forehead from Heather's shoulder, sniffling. Heather grabbed a tissue package from her purse and handed it over with a firm nod.

"You poor thing," Heather whispered. "But they know what they're doing. I have to believe that. Now that they're in conversation with the robbers themselves, they'll figure out a way to end this."

Angie did her best to mop herself up, returning her eyes to the familiar doorway of the Bar Harbor Bank. How many times had she walked up that very walkway, greeting the bank teller on the inside? How many times had she stood at the indoor ATM, gaping at a number that seemed only to go down and down and down?

Ah. Not such a happy memory. But how she wished she could run-up to the door of the bank and howl to the robbers that she understood, in a sense, their plight. Money was the darnedest thing in the world. There was no surviving life without it.

Please. Just let my daughter go. Please.

Suddenly, Paul marched from the cops back toward Angie, Heather, and Luke. With his hands in his pockets, he looked powerful and stoic— the sort of man you wanted in charge of a hostage situation. Angie blinked at him, incredulous.

"What's going on?" Angie demanded. The crime tape between them flickered in the wind.

Paul spoke with urgency, his voice low. "I need to speak with you privately, Angie."

Angie's throat tightened. She turned to look at Luke, the only family she had in the world. "I need my brother with me."

Paul grimaced but nodded, lifting the crime tape to allow only Angie and Luke to slip under. They followed him to the side of the barricaded area, where Paul turned to face away from the crowd. It was almost as though he didn't want anyone to read his lips.

"We've been in contact with the perpetrators within the bank," he explained.

Luke and Angie held the silence. Angie's knees knocked together with fear. Maybe she would explode if he didn't tell her whatever it was immediately. Maybe she'd just die right there on the pavement.

"It seems that your daughter has gone into early labor," Paul added softly, his chocolate eyes drooping.

Angie's lips parted with horror. A million thoughts raced through her mind. Most of all, though, she couldn't get over her anger. This impossibly pivotal moment of going into labor was supposed to be a joyous one. Hannah had discussed it so often with tears in her eyes— fearful yet wide-eyed with optimism. With the due date about four weeks away, they'd discussed several times what to put in an overnight bag, but hadn't yet gotten around to packing anything.

Yet now, Hannah had had to go into labor in front of a crowded bank of hostages and several bank robbers.

How terribly cruel.

"I want to scream," Angie seethed suddenly, gasping for air. Her hands were in fists. "I want to scream and scream and—"

Paul placed his hands on her upper arms and inhaled deeply, nodding for her to follow along. Angie wanted to tell him that she didn't believe in hokey meditation stuff, that if her body wanted to have a panic attack, she would go ahead and let it.

"Come on," Paul assured her. "You have to stay with me here. You can't break down. Not right now. No matter how much you want to."

Angie wanted to tell him just how convenient that sounded.

"Do you understand that my daughter is in the most frightening position of her life?" Angie whispered.

Paul nodded firmly. "The perpetrators have no interest in keeping your daughter inside the bank."

Angie's heart softened. She stumbled forward, as though her legs had given up on her. "What?"

"I don't think they knew your daughter was in the bank today when they burst in," Paul continued. "When they realized she was pregnant, the cracks began to form in their plan. I have a hunch that when she actually went into labor, the perpetrators began to turn on one another. They're having doubts."

"But it's not like they'll just give up," Angie muttered. "There are so many cops out here. And you..." She furrowed her brow, incredulous. "Who are you, Paul?"

Paul waved a hand. "I don't have time to explain. I will say that I have a lot of experience with this sort of thing, with a great track record of getting people back to safety. Okay?"

Angie's throat tightened. It was hard to align the vision of the fantastic drummer she'd hired only nine days ago with the firm and courageous man before her.

"You—you've gotten hostages out of situations like this before?" Her voice no longer sounded like her own.

Paul's eyes were reassuring, like anchors keeping her safe at shore.

"Listen, Angie. I need you to call the ambulance and explain the situation," Paul breathed. "That your daughter will be out of the bank very soon and that she'll need to be taken to the hospital to be closely monitored. We need the ambulance waiting."

Angie inhaled sharply as she nodded. "Yes. Yes, of course." She eyed the door to the bank. Behind there, three criminals stalked with flashing guns, terrifying Hannah to bits. Angie had read stories of mothers lifting cars from their babies; she'd read of mothers storming into burning buildings and retrieving their young. Right then, she felt the power of all those women— yet knew that if she stormed the bank just then, she put far more than just herself in danger. She had to trust Paul's instincts without knowing, even in the slightest, why he had them in the first place.

"Hey, Paul?" Officer Brad appeared beside him with his phone lifted. "He wants to talk to you again. Do you mind?"

"I'll be right there," Paul affirmed. He then cupped Angie's hand tenderly and said those six words, the words that seemed to matter both nothing and everything at once. "She's going to be all right."

Angie grabbed her phone to find yet another message from Fletcher Baxter. She didn't bother to read it and instead found herself dialing 9-1-1 for the first time in her entire life. When she greeted the telephone operator, a power filled her heart, her lungs, her stomach.

"I need an ambulance at the downtown Bar Harbor Bank immediately," she informed her. "My daughter is one of the hostages. And she's going into early labor."

Chapter Seventeen

After more than an hour in the hostage situation, the personalities of the bank robbers had grown incredibly clear. Understanding the nature of their relationships was the only way Hannah could possibly push herself through the brevity and fear of the situation. It was her only distraction.

What she'd gleaned thus far was this.

The loudest guy, the guy who'd been behind the counter screaming at the bank teller about how much money was in the bank, thought himself to be the leader. He was the loudest, the most arrogant— and, if Hannah had to guess, the entire operation had been his idea. From the way he moved and the way he spoke, Hannah had to guess he was somewhere in his mid-to-late thirties.

The other two seemed a bit younger, perhaps mid-to-late twenties. Two of them had similar scratchy voices and accents, which made Hannah guess that they were brothers or cousins. The other was taller, lankier, and somehow clumsier all at once. He was also softer-spoken than the elder brother and the younger brother. When he lifted his gun, he did so half-heart-edly, as though he'd accidentally woken up and found himself in the midst of a bank robbery.

The lanky guy seemed to take the most issue with Hannah's labor, as well. He muttered to the younger brother frequently, whispering so quietly that neither Hannah nor the older leader could understand. All the while, the lanky guy's eyes were upon Hannah as Hannah seethed and puffed her cheeks and tried her hardest to remember everything she'd learned at that stupid Lamaze class.

It seemed unclear to both the bank robbers and all other onlookers who, exactly, was best at speaking with whoever they were in conversation with outside. Over the previous ten minutes or so, the "leader" had been on the phone, making a list of demands that, to Hannah, seemed out of this world. Throughout, the lanky guy and the younger brother watched the hostages on either side of the bank, their shoulders slumped.

"Psst." This was Sharon, off to Hannah's right.

Hannah cast Sharon a harsh look. *Hadn't Sharon heard what the robbers had told them?* There was to be no conversing with one another. Hannah wasn't willing to put the life of her baby at risk just to talk to Sharon.

"Pssst! Hey!"

Hannah winced as a wave of pain rolled over her. She groaned and allowed a single howl to escape her lips before trapping them shut again. On cue, her water broke. A puddle appeared around her thighs, soaking her.

"Oh. No. This won't do," Sharon muttered to herself. She then twisted her head toward the lanky bank robber. Appar-ently, everyone else had figured out that he was the "kind" one (if a kind bank robber was something that existed).

"Excuse me, sir? The pregnant woman's water just broke.

Are you going to force her to sit in her own water until you figure out what's what?" Sharon glowered angrily.

Hannah had to admit that she hadn't thought Sharon had such bravery in her.

The lanky bank robber seized up. He took stock of Hannah and the wet spot forming, then eyed the shorter younger brother robber and said, "You have to help me move her."

"What? No." The younger robber eyed his older brother, who still had the phone locked to his ear.

"Come on, man. There's no telling how much longer this is going to take," the lanky guy growled.

The older guy began to scream into the phone. "You have to stop treating me like I'm a little kid! I told you. I want to speak to the other guy. The Paul guy. He gets me. You idiots don't understand me at all."

Had Hannah not been in such tremendous pain, she might have laughed at the concept of a bank robber feeling "misunderstood."

With the older guy more preoccupied, however, the younger brother and the lanky robber stepped toward Hannah and helped her shift toward the corner, away from the wet spot. Hannah chose not to look at it and instead closed her eyes, remembering a time in kindergarten when she'd accidentally wet her pants. Her initial shame had fallen away so swiftly, mostly because the other kids had been so understanding. *When you're five years old, wetting your pants is just a thing that happens. There's a lot of empathy there.*

In some ways, the sympathy from the robbers reminded her of that moment. Life was a funny thing.

Bar Harbor Bank had several branded sweatshirts and t-shirts hanging in the front foyer of the bank itself. Hannah had always laughed at that, wondering what type of person bought bank t-shirts. In the past, she remembered seeing at least three other Bar Harbor residents with bank t-shirts, proudly championing the branch that safeguarded their money. Hannah had laughed and said, "Hey. I'm not in the big city anymore. The rules are different."

But now, the lanky bank robber splayed one of those sweatshirts across the ground and helped Hannah shift onto it as a way to keep dry. Hannah's eyes watered, although she refused to cry. If she had to have her baby on the damn bank floor in front of Sharon, three bank robbers, and a bunch of other randoms, she'd do it with a proud smile and motherly strength. She didn't want to let the fear set in.

"God, I don't know anything about delivering babies," the younger brother muttered to the lanky one.

"I wish he'd let one of us talk to this guy Paul," the lanky robber said back.

"He's a control freak. What do you expect?" the younger said.

The older guy howled into the phone and staggered back behind the counter, where he placed his elbows down on the countertop. "But that's the thing, Paul! That's exactly what I can't do! I know, the girl is pregnant. I know that. But don't you think that gives me a little bit of leeway here?"

"Dammit, Reggie," the lanky bank robber cursed. "That wasn't a part of the plan."

"We need to get her out," the younger guy muttered angrily. "This isn't funny anymore. Her water just broke!"

Many years ago, Hannah had adored it when the guys had fought over her. "I want to sit next to Hannah," they'd argued with each other, angry that Hannah gave any attention to anyone other than them.

This, admittedly, wasn't as exciting.

Suddenly, the older guy lifted his chin and glared at the younger robber. "I'm sorry. What did you say?" He moved the phone a bit further from his ear, eyeing his younger brother dangerously. "You want to repeat yourself, Bobby?"

Bobby. Reggie. Hannah wanted to remember their names. She eyed the lanky one, curious about his. She'd tell the cops that he was the "good one." She'd tell them that he got caught up in something he shouldn't have.

Well, maybe.

If she got out of there.

The older guy was still screaming at his younger brother. "Didn't I tell you to pay attention to me? Didn't I tell you to trust me?"

"Reggie, come on. The girl's in labor. Me and Rex have no idea how to deliver a baby. Do you?" Bobby demanded.

Reggie. Bobby. Rex. They sounded like the members of a bad punk band.

Reggie howled back at his brother, telling him that they needed this. "Do you have any other ideas on how to get this money? Huh? Didn't I tell you that I'd take care of this? Huh?"

Hannah closed her eyes again as a wave of pain crashed over her abdomen. The water from her breakage caught the light from the overhead lamps. On the far end of the bank, an older man whimpered feebly, his eyes to the ceiling. Hannah's heart broke for all of them. They would never get over this.

But with the bank robbers distracted with their anger, whoever listened on the other end of the phone saw an opening.

It all happened very quickly. Suddenly, someone kicked the front door down and howled, "Get down!" A gun pointed into the space, directly at Reggie. Rex and Bobby both fell to the ground, protecting their own heads with the flats of their hands.

"I said get down!" The man who'd burst through cried, his gun still pointed toward Reggie. "And put the gun where I can see it. Now!"

Reggie's hands shook. His eyes, which were all you could see behind his ski mask, were wide and frightened. Very, very slowly, he lifted his gun to the side, walked around the counter, and positioned it on the ground at his feet.

Hannah's heart pounded. She returned her gaze to the man with the gun, who'd broken in when he'd recognized there was an opening.

Wait. This man was familiar.

Could it be the new drummer of her mother's jazz ensemble?

Hannah's jaw dropped open for a split second before another wave of pain crashed over her. Before she fully knew what had happened, two other police officers entered and fell on either side of her, as two others maintained their position with guns at the front of the bank. As the contraction subsided, a cop asked her if she was all right to walk. She nodded, gripping his elbow as he helped her to her feet.

Hannah staggered toward the doorway, inhaling the fresh air. The gray light that slid through the summertime clouds seemed to be from God himself. An ambulance siren screamed out somewhere by the street, and a huge crowd of people had gathered, set aside from the bank with police tape.

It looked like something in a movie.

Suddenly, Angie appeared before Hannah. Her cheeks were blotchy, and her eyes were rimmed red with tears. Only her smile seemed sure. She wrapped her arms around Hannah and guided her away from the throngs of people toward the flashing red lights.

It took Hannah a long while to hear herself, but when she did, she was muttering, "Oh, Mom. Oh, Mom. Oh, Mom. I was so scared. I was so, so scared."

She seemed to say this over and over again, overwhelmed by the trauma of the past hour.

All the while, her mother whispered back, "I know, baby. But you're going to be all right. I promise you that."

The EMT workers guided Hannah onto a stretcher and eased the stretcher into the back of the ambulance. Hannah had never been in the back of an ambulance before. She eyed the strange machines and tubes. The scary-looking equipment was meant to keep strangers alive. Her mother leaped into the ambulance with her and held her hand.

"We're going to check your vital signs, Hannah. All right?" Someone asked her this, although Hannah had begun to cry, and cry hard, which meant that she couldn't fully see who spoke. She nodded, closing her eyes so that tears drifted down her cheeks.

"I just don't want her to be scared, Mom," Hannah breathed, her heart seizing with worry. "I don't want her to live in that kind of world."

Angie squeezed her hand, letting out a single sob. "We can never fully protect our children, Hannah. All we can do is do the best we can."

"It's not good enough," Hannah howled.

Angie dropped her head alongside Hannah's and kissed her ear, her cheek. "You will always be enough for her. Our love will always be enough. And I'll be right here for the both of you, every step of the way. I promise you that."

Chapter Eighteen

How had Hannah known, in the ambulance, to call her baby a "her"? This was a question Angie only remembered to ask hours later when Hannah was deep in the throngs of delivering her baby girl. Angie decided to table it for later.

Throughout the long and painful process, Angie did what she could to remind Hannah that she wasn't alone in this. Yes, these were horrific circumstances— but together, they would find a way to fight through. Hours after the baby was born, Angie had to take pain medicine, all to relieve the throbbing ache of her hand. It was worth it.

The baby girl was perfect. Healthy, gorgeous, with ten fingers and ten toes and bright blue eyes. It was hard to remember that, genetically, she was fifty percent of that loser Hannah had dated out in Chicago. When the thought came through Angie's mind, she immediately dismissed it. He had nothing to do with their lives now.

Hannah was exhausted and clearly thrilled to pieces. She kept whispering to her daughter just how perfect she was.

"Don't let anyone tell you anything different," she whispered, her eyes welling with tears.

Eventually, Hannah slept. The baby, still unnamed, did as well. Angie remained tireless. She wandered the hallways of the hospital, sipping water and side-eyeing the other hospital visitors there in the labor and delivery wing. Most everyone seemed somewhere between euphoric and terrified and completely exhausted. She wished a young couple "congratulations," watching their love blossom over the birth of a baby. It ached to remember her own first moments as a mother with her ex by her side.

It was one in the morning. Very soon, it would be twenty-four hours after the hostage situation had begun. It was difficult for Angie to remember just how long the labor and delivery had been. Out of curiosity, she asked the nurse on duty, who checked the chart and reported that the baby's birth had taken a full nine hours after they'd checked in.

"What a trooper," the nurse beamed.

"You have no idea," Angie breathed.

The nurse cocked her head. "Wait. Is this the hostage baby?"

Angie glowered at her, a protective mother unwilling to discuss the privacy of her daughter's life. The nurse got the hint and disappeared down the hall, probably thinking about the insanity of all mothers. She was allowed to think that. It was the truth, after all.

All mothers could be insane, overwhelmed with the immensity of their love. Angie was proud of that.

When Angie returned to the waiting room to grab another cup of coffee somewhere around three, she was surprised to find a familiar face. Paul sat in one of the plastic chairs, his body thrown forward, his head between his legs. He'd removed his bulletproof vest, yet still seemed a tower of a man, filled with a power that Angie didn't fully understand.

She had the strangest desire to kiss him, yet let the emotion die on the vine.

"Paul?" Angie dropped on a chair across the waiting room from him, too afraid to get closer. She had seen him brandish a gun earlier that day.

It had been a remarkable thing.

Paul lifted his head and then jumped with surprise, bringing his shoulders back. It was almost like he didn't want her to see him that weak. She shook her head, wordless. How could she even begin to thank him?

And finally, she figured out the perfect way.

"The baby is healthy," she whispered.

Paul's shoulders slumped again. He looked so relieved. "God, it's so good to hear that."

"Hannah and baby are resting," Angie continued, her voice catching. "Baby is as yet unnamed. But she's a girl." Her heart welled at that. She hadn't known how much she'd wanted a girl. A granddaughter.

After a dramatic pause, Angie nodded. "It's your turn to tell me what happened."

Paul clenched his eyes. "The perpetrators are in custody. After extensive interviews, all hostages have been cleared to go home."

"You were remarkable today, Paul." Angie's voice broke. She hadn't expected herself to compliment him so readily.

Paul grimaced. "I don't know about that." He swallowed, then added, "One of the bank robbers had a fake gun."

"And the other two?" Angie whispered.

Paul nodded. "I can't understand why this guy went along with it and still brought a fake gun. It's like he didn't want to be to blame if something went wrong."

Angie squeezed her eyes shut, fully facing the horrific reality that her daughter had been at gunpoint only hours before. She would never get over it. None of them would.

"We learned their motive. The bank didn't clear a loan for one of them. The older guy," Paul continued. "He was going to lose his wife, his children, and his house."

Angie didn't know what to say.

"I'm not saying you should pity him in the slightest," Paul affirmed.

Angie coughed. Her head swam with sudden fatigue. "But it is true that I know what it's like to feel like the entire world is against you."

Paul tilted his head. He knew nothing about her, not really. They'd met only ten days ago.

"I'd better get going," he told her softly. "I guess there's no convincing you that you should go home and rest."

"No way," Angie affirmed with a soft smile. After a pause, she added, "And no convincing you to tell me where the heck you came from?"

What kind of work had he done? Where did he come from? Why had a hostage situation seemed like second nature to him? The questions piled on top of one another.

"Not today," Paul offered sadly. He rose to his feet, adjusting his black jeans.

"You haven't been home since before jazz practice, have you?"

"It doesn't matter." He sniffed and reached into his back pocket, drawing out his drumsticks. Impossibly, they'd been there the entire time. "I guess I'll see you at rehearsal later this week?"

"I wouldn't miss it for the world."

"Good. Me neither." Paul gave her a final nod and turned on a heel, walking away from her and into the shadows of the hospital hallways. Very soon, he was out of sight.

* * *

"Half a day old." Angie held the tiniest of all babies in her arms, cradling her as Hannah looked on, crossing and uncrossing her arms anxiously. Hannah and the baby had only just awoken that morning at six, no more than twenty-five minutes ago, and both were bright-eyed and slightly confused. Angie could fix that. She could fix anything.

"Did you sleep?" Hannah asked softly.

Angie ignored her daughter, locking eyes with her grand-daughter. Her lips were supple, her cheeks the softest things in the world. She kicked her feet gently, just as she had when she'd been in Hannah's stomach.

"A name came to me," Hannah breathed.

Angie lifted her eyes to her daughter's. "Oh?"

Hannah nodded, her smile electric. Angie half-expected Hannah to come out with something absolutely insane, like "Seraphina" or "Webber" or "Aaaslayan" or whatever young people were naming their children these days. Angie waited with bated breath.

And then, like a song, Hannah came out with, "Sophie."

Angie's heart cracked into a million pieces. "Sophie. I love it."

Hannah nodded, her cheeks bulging. There was no way to bottle what this young mother felt for her young one. Angie stood and returned her baby, watching as Hannah swooned with love. God, to be young, God, to be in love. God, to be brand-new in the world. Angie, in her late forties, suddenly felt ancient.

The hospital's visiting hours began at ten that morning. The first to arrive were Luke and Heather, who doted on baby Sophie joyously and wrapped Angie in big hugs. Heather said that Nicole hadn't known what to do all afternoon and had "baked up a storm."

"When you get home, you have a whole lot of cookies to get

through," she warned Hannah and Angie. "I hope you're all right with that."

"More than all right," Hannah affirmed. "I just lost so much weight. I need to gain it back."

Everyone chuckled, their eyes dancing. Hannah could charm the pants off of anyone. It was simply her way.

After Heather and Luke left, Abby and Nicole scampered in. Abby flung herself at her business partner and newfound best friend, crying, "I should never have let you go to the bank by yourself!"

But Hannah brushed this off. "Girl, please. In the future, when we're at parties trying to impress people with stories, I'll be like— I was a hostage once! What will you say?"

Abby groaned. "You're right. I'm so boring."

"My point exactly," Hannah affirmed, her eyes sparkling.

Obviously, everyone knew she was joking, that the immensity of this trauma was difficult to gauge. But she was all right. Her baby was all right. That's all that mattered. Well, that, and good humor.

"Oh, and the best part of it is? I'm not pregnant anymore," Hannah said excitedly. "I can finally run around our events, taking photographs. We'll be unstoppable."

Abby laughed. "You can't be serious."

"Why not?"

"I don't know. Most mothers take real time off after childbirth?" Abby eyed her mother and Angie wide-eyed. "Right?"

Hannah waved a hand. "I'll be right as rain in a couple of weeks."

Abby turned to face baby Sophie, who slept soundly on her mother's chest. "Sophie, what do you think about this?"

"Sorry, my other business partner is out of the office at the moment," Hannah teased. "So, I guess that means you'll have to speak directly to me."

Abby groaned. "Just promise me you'll think about your health first and foremost."

"Yeah, yeah. All right." Hannah stuck out her tongue, clearly pleased.

A few more moments passed. Abby shifted her weight.

"Out with it, Abs. I can always tell when there's something on your mind. What's up?"

Abby grimaced. Finally, she said, "I don't want to talk about it. Not too much. But I wanted to tell you that the suitcase was discovered at the bank, untouched. We should be able to claim it as ours."

Hannah's grin was nourishing and alive. "That is brilliant news."

Abby's eyes glistened. "It really is."

The following hour of visitation was truly joyous. Casey and Grant arrived, as did Ashlee and Marvin from the jazz ensemble. Everyone doted on baby Sophie, counting her toes and squealing over her adorable cheeks and full eyes.

By the end of visitation, both Hannah and Sophie had fallen back into the throes of slumber, leaving an exhausted Angie to bid goodbye to Marvin and Ashlee alone. When they finally disappeared down the hall, she crumbled into a ball on a nearby chair and fell into a deep sleep. She didn't wake for a number of hours.

Thank goodness.

Chapter Nineteen

A**NGIE: It's been the most shocking week of my life. My daughter was held hostage at gunpoint. After that, she went into labor and was taken immediately to the hospital, where she gave birth to a healthy, beautiful baby girl. We're so in love! And so exhausted, all at once.**

Angie placed her phone back on the kitchen table, filled with fear. A towel was flung across her shoulder, and a strange, rank smell came up from her armpits, proof she hadn't had time to shower in two days' time. Baby Sophie was now four days old and slept like a log, as most newborns do. Angie felt like a new parent all over again as she'd helped Hannah change diapers, burp baby Sophie and pick up the slack any way she could. Even though she was foreign to this new world, she absolutely adored being a new grandma.

Angie padded into the nursery to find Hannah in the rocking chair with a sleeping Sophie in her arms. Hannah gave her mother a soft smile.

"Did you write him?" she whispered.

Angie nodded. Dread stirred in her gut. "I hope it wasn't too much? You told me not to write him long messages."

Hannah shrugged. "I think this week deserves long messages."

Angie groaned and dropped to the ground, crossing her legs and gazing at Sophie. Her heart surged with love. "Who'd have thought such a beautiful, peaceful baby could create so much noise?"

Hannah giggled quietly, carefully. Still, she wasn't done discussing the text message. "Besides. If he doesn't appreciate the craziness of this week, then what kind of guy is he?"

"Not my kind of guy, I suppose." Angie's stomach twisted. "I just feel bad that I ignored him for so many days."

"Didn't he ignore you, too?"

Angie shrugged. Hannah shrugged back. They shared a brief chuckle before Hannah asked, "What about Paul?"

Angie shook her head. "What about him?"

"I don't know. He just seems like a really excellent guy."

"I don't even know him," Angie pointed out.

"Not that you know this other guy, either," Hannah shot back.

Angie rolled her eyes, sharing a smile. "Touché." She adjusted a strand behind her ear, then added, "Your dad got the divorce papers."

Hannah puffed out her cheeks. "You heard from him?"

"He wants to talk to you."

"Of course he does." Hannah's eyes swam with tears. "I don't know when I'll be ready. Maybe soon. Like, when she graduates from high school."

Angie swallowed the lump in her throat, overwhelmed. "Don't let it go that long, honey. Please. Time is all we have. You know?"

A little while later, Fletcher wrote back.

FLETCHER BAXTER: Hi! Good to hear from you.

FLETCHER BAXTER: Wow, what a wild week you've had. I have to admit, I heard about that hostage situation over in Bar Harbor. Never could have guessed that you were involved.

FLETCHER BAXTER: Congratulations on your granddaughter! What a remarkable feeling that must be.

FLETCHER BAXTER: I'd love to see you. I'm sure it's a challenging time right now.

Angie fell back on the floor of the nursery, reading the message over and over again. His heart surged with excitement. In the rocking chair, Hannah groaned.

"You're obsessed. You're no better than a twenty-year-old girl."

ANGIE: When could you come to Bar Harbor?

To this, Fletcher began to type. Angie knew this based on the "FLETCHER IS TYPING" text across her phone. But over the next two hours, that "FLETCHER IS TYPING" appeared, then disappeared, then reappeared again, all without any sort of answer. Angie didn't want to bother her daughter with questions about his behavior. Instead, after she ensured Hannah and Sophie were all right for the night, she disappeared into her own bedroom, placed her face on the pillow, and wept.

She couldn't say exactly what made her cry so hard.

Probably, it all had to do with relief. Hannah was safe. Sophie had arrived into the world without a scrape on her. The future was bright. She couldn't give power to this handsome man, Fletcher. He was probably busy, unsure of how to fit her into the chaos of his life. That was reasonable, wasn't it?

Toward midnight, Fletcher finally wrote back.

FLETCHER BAXTER: I've put you down for my party on August 6. So looking forward to seeing you perform again.
FLETCHER BAXTER: Sleep well, darling.
FLETCHER BAXTER: Goodnight.

Chapter Twenty

The next week and a half passed in a flurry of activity. There were diapers to change, lactation specialists to visit, and band rehearsals to maintain. On top of it all, Angie had to find a way to care for herself— to feed herself and put herself to sleep, despite the anxiety of her innermost soul.

On the morning of August 6th, Angie awoke to discover Hannah and Sophie already awake. From the doorway of the nursery, Angie sipped her coffee and peered in to watch her daughter sing soft songs to Sophie, who buzzed her lips along with each tune as though she'd known them forever.

"Oh. I didn't see you!" Hannah lifted her eyes, her cheeks flushing with embarrassment.

Angie waved a hand. "I didn't want to interrupt."

Hannah laughed. "I've become a lame mother, haven't I?"

"You have not. If singing to your newborn makes you lame, then all mothers are," Angie insisted. "It's par for the course."

A beat passed. Sophie filled the silence with her adorable

coos. Both Hannah and Angie already knew it was too late for both of them. Sophie had them wrapped around her tiny finger.

"You leave at eleven?" Hannah asked.

"The party begins around three," Angie affirmed.

"You nervous to see your beau?" Hannah asked.

Angie's cheeks burned with embarrassment. "It'll be strange but good to see him. I feel like we've been dancing around this for a while."

"That's what dating is," Hannah offered with a shrug. "At least, that's what I remember of it. I won't be out there dating for a long, long time. Will I, Sophie?" She sang the last part joyously, turning her eyes back to her darling daughter. Angie had a funny jolt of a memory, those long-lost days when Hannah had "kept her" from living her normal life. She'd had to turn down dinner parties and musician outings, and late-night talks with Chicago-based composers. Secretly, it had thrilled her to abandon her normal life to build that other one with Hannah. She wasn't sure there was anything better.

Angie returned to the kitchen and stuck a slice of whole-grain toast into the toaster. She sipped her coffee, watching for the toast before it sprung out, browned and hot. From the nursery, Hannah called out, "Yes, please!" Grinning to herself, Angie prepared the toast the way Hannah had always liked it: covered with butter, cinnamon, and the slightest bit of sugar.

Angie delivered two slices of cinnamon toast to the nursery, where Hannah promised that she would "really limit her sugar intake, eventually," now that she was a mother. Both Angie and Hannah knew this wasn't the truth.

Angie showered beneath a shower head that seemed to produce less pressure as each day passed. The water dribbled across her shoulder blades and across her scalp. After she'd gotten most of the shampoo suds from her hair, she stepped onto the bathroom mat and rubbed the towel across her chest, her shoulders, and her legs. Just as she'd done since she was a girl, she avoided the mirror, too anxious to engage with her own reflection. She often wondered if other women were like that—too frightened of the reality of their aging face to engage with it.

She dressed in a black dress with a surging neckline, one that Hannah had called "provocative but also classy." She then did her makeup, her hand shaking chaotically as she attempted to line her eyes with liquid black. How on earth did women learn to doll themselves up? To Angie, it would remain a mystery forever.

The group chat for the jazz ensemble began to explode with excitement for the afternoon ahead.

ASHLEE: Guys, I just searched for this mansion online. It's immaculate. Apparently, a movie was filmed there a few years ago? Some movie called 'Lights Out'?

MARVIN: Wait. THAT mansion? That's where the party is?

Angie had never heard of that movie, nor had she researched the site of the party. According to the emails and texts she'd exchanged with Fletcher, the property upon which the party was to take place belonged to Fletcher's father.

FLETCHER: The old man's agreed to give me full reign of his estate, if you can believe it.

FLETCHER: Perhaps you can tell by my tone— my father and I have never seen eye-to-eye. That said, he has a real eye for property, for homes. And I can't wait to share this place with you.

It had been decided that the members of the jazz ensemble would carpool. Ashlee and Marvin hovered outside in a minivan at five past eleven, waving their hands wildly from the front seat. When Angie leaped inside, she discovered the bassist, Hank, wearing a thick pair of sunglasses and giving her a funny nod. He looked sleepy-eyed and slightly stoned, not that Angie could ever really tell when someone had smoked marijuana. It wasn't her business, anyway.

"The others are waiting for us at the on-ramp to the highway," Marvin explained from the front seat. "Well, everyone else except Paul."

Angie's heart surged. "How is Paul getting there?"

Ashlee waved a hand. "Paul marches to the beat of his own drum. Get it?" She guffawed, then wrinkled her nose.

"Oh, Ashlee. That was awful," Marvin teased. "Can you keep your bad jokes to yourself? Just for once?"

"The doctor said that if I try to keep them inside, I might injure myself," Ashlee quipped.

Since Paul had dropped by the hospital very early the morning after Sophie's birth, Angie had seen Paul only three times— each time at rehearsal, only. Throughout each practice session, he'd seemed unwilling to meet her eye, as though they'd fallen into the depths of overly intense intimacy.

"Everyone's talking about Paul," Ashlee continued, sipping her coffee as she glanced back toward Angie. "He was like a cowboy in a western movie."

Angie grimaced as Ashlee continued to take stock of her.

"Did he tell you anything about his background?" Ashlee continued to dig.

"He mentioned he had a lot of experience with stuff like that," Angie breathed, "But he didn't seem willing to say much else."

"A mysterious guy," Ashlee said.

"Maybe he's ex-military?" Marvin guessed.

"Or in the CIA," Hank added.

Angie hated the sensation of gossiping about Paul. She dropped her gaze to her kneecaps and waited for the conversation to shift. It soon did, especially as they whipped past the other members of the jazz ensemble. The driver, the trombonist named Megan, beeped the horn in greeting. They were on their way.

"This guy never told you what kind of party it was?" Ashlee asked a few minutes later.

Angie wanted to make something up, to lie. "He said something about impressing his business associates."

"Any idea what he does?" Ashlee asked.

Angie was stumped. Hadn't they covered this sort of information? Fletcher was clearly powerful, steeped in money.

"Maybe he's CIA," Marvin joked with the snap of his fingers.

Ashlee cackled, punching Marvin's upper arm lightly. In the back seat, however, Hank nodded, his eyes shadowed with seriousness. "You might have something there," he said.

* * *

They arrived at the mansion on the outskirts of Portland at one forty-five in the afternoon. Ashlee whistled to herself as Marvin shut off the engine.

"Are you impressed? We made good time," Marvin said, gesturing toward the clock.

Ashlee rolled her eyes. "Why do men always want to talk about the 'good time' they make? I'm just glad we got here safe and sound."

Angie stepped out of the side of the van and blinked toward the splendorous sight: a gorgeous nineteenth-century mansion built with red brick and dark green shutters. A massive porch wrapped around the house, harkening back to long-ago afternoons when its families had gathered to watch the world go by.

The mansion's surroundings had been decorated elaborately. Gardens exploded with life, flashing their bright yellow petals and their thick green stalks beneath the summer sun.

"Is that the band?" An event planner with a traditional event-planner clipboard approached, wearing a doubtful smile.

"We are, indeed," Angie said.

The woman marked something on her clipboard and gestured for them to follow her. "I'll have you set up near the white tables," she explained, pointing to a dining area nearest the rose gardens. "You're providing dinner music, after all. It's only fitting." She sniffed and jotted something else on her clipboard. Angie guessed the woman just wanted to seem busier than she actually was. It was a gift.

Together, the jazz ensemble began to set up their chairs and the keyboard that Angie had brought from home. As they worked, Paul parked his car as close to the rose garden as he could and began to carry pieces of his drum set over, holding the pieces of metal awkwardly as he went.

"How was your drive?" Angie asked Paul, leaning against her keyboard and watching as he screwed little pieces of the drum set together.

Paul froze for a long moment, tilting his head as he inspected a screw on the set. "Not bad. And yours?"

The words stung. *How was it possible that someone could show such density to their soul to you and then immediately recede into darkness again?*

Angie couldn't bring herself to answer. Instead, she turned to face the rest of her musicians, clapping her hands together. "I'm going to head inside to use the bathroom and say hello to our client."

Ashlee lifted a big thumb. Marvin squawked on his saxophone, which made Ashlee cackle. Angie swept her hair behind her ears and walked purposefully through the white tables, past the rose garden, and then around, where a large floor had been set up, surrounded by stereos. An ornate sign sat outside the side entrance of the elaborate mansion, advertising the location of the bathroom. Thank goodness.

Angie stepped into the dark shadows of the mansion. Each footfall echoed from wall to wall, ricocheting through the back corners and across the old-world paintings and down the long hallways that seemed to lead to a thousand impossibly beautiful worlds. Angie followed the signs for the bathroom, which was an elaborate women-only suite with chaise lounges, ornate couches, antique mirrors, and an old-fashioned powdering station. It felt like stepping back in time.

Had Fletcher actually grown up in this house, surrounded by such wealth? How had Angie grabbed his attention? The dress she'd worn on the night they'd met one another had cost thirteen dollars in a second-hand shop.

Angie used the bathroom and then stepped into the salon area, searching her purse for her heinous liquid eyeliner. It needed a touch-up. As she leaned toward the mirror, several women dressed in black catering clothes burst into the women's area. They cackled joyously, drawing their fingers across the marble of the sink. They all seemed to be in their twenties, probably putting themselves through school with whatever money they earned catering.

"Get a load of this place, Kathy," one of the girls howled. "There's no way they see it anymore. Can't appreciate what they've always had."

Kathy scoffed, grabbing a lipstick and drawing it around and around her lips. Already, she looked like Ronald McDonald.

"Ugh, that guy is such a jerk," the first girl moaned. "I told him our policy about the down payment, and he literally laughed in my face. I mean, the guy has more money than God."

Angie stiffened. *Was this about Fletcher?* Her heart burned with curiosity. Her ears ringing, she turned to catch her eye and asked, "I'm sorry. Hi. I'm in the band performing at dinner."

"Oh." The girl blushed and capped her lipstick. "Hired help. Like us. Good to meet you."

Angie's smile felt frozen. "I wondered who you were talking about."

The girl waved her hand. "Oh, you know. The old guy who owns this mansion. I should have known not to take this gig."

"Why's that?" Angie asked.

The girl's eyes widened to saucers. "He owns like half the banks in the state of Maine. While so, so many people in Maine go hungry or lose their homes or lose their jobs, this fat cat has this enormous house and plenty of cash to throw around for his bratty son's wedding..."

Angie's eyebrow leaped to her hairline. "I'm sorry. Which bratty son?"

The caterer waved a tired hand. "This wedding. I heard it cost upward of one hundred grand. How much are you charging to perform here? Curious."

Angie's throat filled with phlegm. She backed toward the door, her thoughts whirling. This was obviously an enormous misunderstanding. Hadn't Fletcher said that he had a brother somewhere?

"Okay. Don't tell me." the caterer said with a flippant shrug. She then uncapped her lipstick and continued to perform her lipstick ritual as Kathy shifted her weight beside her, sucking in her stomach to show off for the mirror.

Angie burst out into the heat of the afternoon. Pit stains formed in her black dress, unseen by others yet weighing Angie down. She bucked toward a long and beautifully decorated table, feeling somewhere outside of her body. There, at the center of the table, sat a massive cake— complete with a couple atop it, their hands locked to symbolize their holy matrimony. Forever, they would walk through life side-by-side.

And at the base of the cake, the decorator had written the names of the bride and groom with flourishing cursive.

It was stunning, even in its horror.

For there, in soft lavender icing, read: **JAMIE AND FLETCHER.**

Chapter Twenty-One

It felt like a black-out— as though Angie was eighteen again, too many vodka shots, staggering around a party, and searching for a way home.

Instead, she was a forty-something woman at the wedding of a man she'd thought that, maybe, she could love. As she stared down at the cake, proof that every daydream she'd had was built on lies, her knees buckled beneath her. Someone howled out for help. And a split second later, strong arms lifted her to a nearby chair, where she slung herself over the back and gazed up at the eggshell blue sky.

Abstractly, she wondered if Fletcher had put in an order to God himself for the most beautiful of summer days.

Paul dropped to a squat in front of her. There they were: those chocolate brown eyes again, ready to tether her back to reality.

"What happened over there?" Paul asked, his voice low.

Along the rose bushes, the rest of the jazz ensemble had begun to warm up, thumping into a beautiful jazz beat that had nothing at all to do with the glitz and gloss of Fletcher's wedding to Jamie. Jamie. *Who was Jamie?*

Paul's hands were splayed gently on her knees. Angie blinked at the long, capable fingers at the thick brows that crawled across his forehead.

"It's nothing," she told Paul with a wave of her hand.

"It didn't look like nothing." He blinked once, unwilling to let her go.

Angie's lips parted. Upon her tongue, she held the story that she so needed to explain. If she confessed everything, what would Paul say to her? Would he think she was stupid for falling for someone like Fletcher? Would he think, as she now did, that men like Fletcher were literally born to take advantage of women like Angie?

"We'd better get back to the others," Angie breathed.

Paul tilted his head. Between them, the air sizzled. Angie remembered the way he'd looked that night after the hostage situation, the hollows beneath his eyes as dark as night.

Angie forced herself to stand. With Paul a half-step behind her at all times, she trudged toward the jazz ensemble set-up, where Marvin buzzed at the saxophone reed, his eyes clenched. Angie collapsed on the piano bench as Paul perched at the drum set. They locked eyes for a split second before Paul's head dropped forward and his drumsticks took flight. With that cue, the rest of the jazz ensemble joined it, taking Angie's horrific mood on an emotional and glorious ride. After Marvin improvised through a saxophone solo, Angie took her own solo, her eyes closed as her hands swept easily across the keys. Across the rest of the ensemble, her co-musicians howled and clapped, having never seen their "leader," Angie, fall into the music like that. This, Angie knew, was the beauty of music; it seemed the more heartbroken you were, the more transcendent your playing became. It was a curse and a gift, all at once.

After a little more than fifteen minutes, the guests began to arrive. The event planner, who, Angie now knew, was a "wedding planner" through and through, arrived to explain that the bride enjoyed the jazz ensemble's rehearsal so much that she'd like them to play until all of the guests were seated for the wedding. Angie's eyes became glassy with tears as she took in this information. She then eyed Paul, whose eyes remained confused and sorrowful. He refused to let her off the hook.

"Of course, the bride says that she'll make it worth your while," the wedding planner continued.

Angie's heart seized. Her eyes searched the grounds just beyond the reception area, where, she now saw, Fletcher stood next to another man, smoking cigarettes and speaking intimately, as though they shared secrets.

Was Fletcher bragging about having kissed the pianist, who now performed at his own wedding? Some men were like that, overly braggadocios about their "wins" in the world of romance. They were like conquerors. Angie knew this well. Her ex-husband had been like that, after all.

Angie blinked through the space between herself and Fletcher. He now seemed like a stranger.

Over at his drum set, Paul followed Angie's gaze. A look of understanding passed over his face. Suddenly, he stood up and charged over to the wedding planner and Angie. Angie's fingers grew lax, falling to her thighs. The wedding planner, trained in the art of smiling through all types of pain, continued to grin at Paul. Paul didn't smile back.

"Do you mind if I speak to my colleague for a moment?" Paul asked.

The wedding planner said, "Only a moment. We cannot have more than a sixty-second break between songs. Guests get nervous during the quiet moments." Her smile waned just the slightest bit as she added, "The bride and groom will not take kindly to me if I allow something like that to happen."

"Sixty seconds," Paul affirmed, rapping his knuckles on the

keyboard. "We promise you that."

The wedding planner mumbled to herself, pressed a button on her earpiece, and began to bark instructions to whichever poor soul lurked on the other end of the mic. The tears across Angie's eyes were heavy and threatening to roll down her cheeks.

"You know, Angie," Paul began tenderly, "we don't have to stay here if you feel uncomfortable."

Angie imagined it— a world in which she and the rest of her ensemble packed up their instruments and drove the three hours back to Bar Harbor, all because of her stupid broken heart. She blinked, and finally, a single tear shot toward her cheek.

Finally, Angie lifted her eyes toward his. "I formed this band so that we could perform at this very party."

"You never mentioned anything about a wedding," Paul murmured.

Angie raised her left shoulder a half-inch. "No. Neither did he."

Paul turned his drumsticks over one another. They clunked evenly. "We should pack up immediately. Head home."

He spoke so softly and so sinisterly. Angie thought again of Paul on the phone with the bank robbers before he took an opportunity to charge in and save her daughter's life. He was a force of nature.

"Angie, people who don't appreciate you, don't deserve even a moment of your time," Paul continued to breathe.

But again, Angie considered the weight of her current life.

She remembered the dwindling bank account, her mother's arrival to Maine, and the ache in her back, which had come as a result of a bad second-hand mattress. If there was anything she needed, it was money.

As a mother, she knew better than most that sometimes,

you had to shove away your own emotions in pursuit of a higher mission.

"That man is a sad excuse for a man," Angie whispered, her words harsh. "But I'm a professional. I came here to play with my brand-new jazz ensemble. Playing music like this is still the most powerful medicine in the world. I won't let him take that away from me."

Paul's gaze was a little overwhelming but comforting. Angie had the strangest sensation that she could tell him anything that came to her mind, and he would automatically understand it.

"If you're sure," he said.

"I've never been surer of anything in my life," Angie told him.

"Hey?" The wedding planner popped back out from nowhere and pointed at her wrist, pretending there was a watch there. There wasn't.

Angie gave the woman a half-roll of her eyes, then turned her gaze to her newfound musical family. Paul rushed back to his drum set and counted them out, leading them into "Ain't Misbehavin'," a classic tune that had the wedding guests bouncing and singing as they walked from the parking lot to the wedding site itself.

Throughout, Angie allowed herself a number of piano solos, as though she wanted to prove to Fletcher just how "okay" she was. She felt she could feel his gaze upon her, especially as he stood at the head of the aisle, his hands crossed over his waist as he awaited the beginning of the wedding ceremony itself. Very soon, his bride would approach him all dressed in white. Very soon, they would be pledged man and wife forevermore.

But what the heck did forever mean, anyway?

* * *

The wedding planner announced that the jazz ensemble could take a much-needed break during the ceremony. The other musicians bustled toward the drink table on the far end of the reception area, which offered no view of the wedding ceremony at all. You could almost pretend you were just at a bougie party with the most iconic decorations and the most expensive liquor. You could almost pretend you weren't at the wedding of the man you'd wanted to love.

Angie grabbed a glass of chardonnay and sat at the far edge of a cushioned reception chair, watching her feet. A singer brought the bridesmaids and bride down the aisle; her "Ave Maria" was forgettable yet fine. Paul and the rest of Angie's jazz musicians had more musicality in their little fingers.

"Oh my God." Ashlee arrived back at the reception area after a brief stint in the bathroom. "I saw the bride's dress."

"Shh," Marvin hushed her. "Don't talk so loud. They're just around the corner!"

Ashlee's cheeks burned red with embarrassment. She grabbed a glass of champagne and dropped into the chair beside Angie, her eyes bugging out.

"You probably don't want to know what I have to say," Ashlee offered. "I mean, these people are kind of your friends, right?"

Angie's tongue was parched. She sucked down another bit of wine. "Come on. I love gossip as much as the next woman. Tell me."

Secretly, she was dying to know.

"Oh, it's hideous," Ashlee whispered, her eyes dancing with afternoon sunlight. "It's got all this lace and a long train. Like, rivaling Princess Diana's. And her makeup! I don't know if it's a more modern style. But she looks like she's going to a rave."

"You're kidding," Angie breathed. "None of that goes together."

"I heard the wedding planner say something about it all being, like, 'avant-garde.' Whatever that means," Ashlee said.

Angie sipped her wine and rolled her shoulders back, allowing herself this unique pleasure. No, she wasn't marrying Fletcher. And no, Fletcher had probably never seen her as a viable option. She wasn't from money; she was aging with a flat tire around her middle; she wasn't "hip"; she normally sought out jazz hits from the twentieth century.

That said, she never, in a million years, could have imagined herself selecting anything more hideous than what the bride wore that fateful day. Call it "petty," but Angie decided to take pleasure in it. It was all she had.

* * *

Just as it had at Natalie's wedding, Angie's jazz ensemble's performance during the dinner and the first part of the reception went off without a hitch. Throughout, Angie found herself forgetting about the events of the day and falling completely into the music, her eyes closed as Paul kicked out a beat and Marvin wailed a glorious saxophone solo.

Throughout, Fletcher's guests ate heartily and chatted over the music. The music, then, was for Angie and her co-musicians only. It was their art and their escape. It was what they needed to survive.

Toward the end of their set, Jamie the bride dragged Fletcher over to the ensemble to thank them for all they'd done. Over the course of the dinner, Jamie's makeup had smeared across her face and stained the very top of the lace of her dress. Fletcher stood beside her, sweating profusely.

Angie made a point to stare him directly in the eye as a way to tell him just how little this mattered to her. Unfortunately, he didn't glance her way at all.

"We just can't believe how talented you are," Jamie cried,

clasping both hands around one of Fletcher's. "Thank you so much for being a part of our special day."

"Yes. Thank you." Fletcher's voice sounded stiff and unemotional, entirely unlike the man Angie thought she'd known.

"Oh! And, honey?" Jamie stretched a hand out toward Fletcher, who removed an envelope from his pocket. Jamie placed the envelope across Paul's hand. "Fletcher's father just adored your performance. He added a little something extra to the payment."

Paul looked as though he struggled to smile at her. The muscles in his cheeks failed him.

Lucky for Paul, the rest of the jazz ensemble, minus Angie, hadn't a clue what was going on. They knew, only, that they'd put on a stunning performance and were now getting paid for it. What else could they do but thank Jamie profusely? What else could they do but compliment her and her heinous dress? Throughout, Angie remained quiet, her heart burning within the acid of her stomach.

* * *

After they packed up for the night, Angie followed Paul wordlessly toward his truck and slipped into the driver's seat. A small voice in the back of her mind asked, *"What the heck will the other musicians think?"* But at that moment, she couldn't care less.

She needed him.

Throughout the first part of the drive, Paul and Angie remained wordless. The windows of the truck were down an inch or so, and fresh Maine winds flashed across their cheeks and their foreheads. Angie was reminded of long-ago afternoons, driving across Ohio with her father. The wind seemed like the same wind.

"I worked as a cop, specializing in hostage situations," Paul suddenly said, adjusting his grip across the steering wheel. "In Boston."

Angie's heart pounded. She turned her eyes toward him. There he was, in all his damaged glory— the sharpness of his nose, his unsmiling lips, his chocolate eyes.

"Oh my God," she breathed.

"Yeah." Paul adjusted his collar. "It was intense, to say the least. Bank robberies. Kidnappings. You name it, I've seen it."

Angie's heart pounded. She had no idea what to say next.

"It's why I took up the drums," Paul continued. "I started in that line of work when I was twenty-four. It took a lot out of me, even then. Made me so angry. I had to release that anger somewhere, you know?"

Angie wiped her cheek with the back of her hand. She'd begun to cry again. "You're a damn good drummer," she told him finally.

Paul gave a wry laugh. "Yeah. Well." He shrugged. "I saw a lot of stuff I'll never forget. I like to think you can feel that emotion in the music."

Angie's eyes widened. "I was just thinking the same thing about my own music."

Paul eyed her knowingly. There was a moment of comfortable silence. Angie's fingers twitched. She wanted so desperately to place her hand over his.

"It must have been awful for you to do it all over again," she said. "At the bank in Bar Harbor."

"I couldn't sleep for a few days. It was triggering." He swallowed and dropped his head against the headrest. "But given the chance, I'd do it all over again. The thing is, I have those skills. I'm capable. Just because I retired back in the city doesn't mean that I won't be needed wherever I am."

This time, Angie allowed herself to drape her hand over his. Her heart surged with emotion. For a long, long time, she was wordless. *After all, how could you thank someone, truly, for saving your daughter and granddaughter's life?*

To her surprise, Paul was the one to break the silence.

"Have you ever jammed with just the piano and drums?"

Angie's lips parted with surprise. "Not often. But I have."

Paul lifted his shoulder the slightest bit, as though he'd just asked her something embarrassing— something that had revealed his innermost soul.

"Maybe we could jam together sometime. Just us."

Another tear traced Angie's cheek. Angie couldn't mistake this for anything else than what it was. Against all odds, the quiet and emotionally broken Paul wanted to start anew. And maybe, just maybe, he wanted to do it with her.

"I'd like that very much," Angie whispered, her voice catching. "I think you're one of the best musicians I've ever met. It would be an honor to play alongside you."

Chapter Twenty-Two

"That's it, Mom. Just another few steps." Angie gripped Wendy's upper arm tenderly, watching as her feet crept tentatively across the carpet of the memory wing at the Bar Harbor care facility. On the other side, Luke had Wendy's other arm and wore a painful smile, as though he'd told himself that he just needed to "keep smiling" to get through the pain of the day.

"Here we are." A nurse stepped out of Wendy's brand-new room, opening the door wide to reveal the interior. Although Luke and Angie had seen the space just last week, it was another thing to see it through Wendy's eyes. How much of this could she understand? Did she know that this was probably the final "home" of her life?

Angie shoved this thought away, refusing to give it power. They would cross that bridge when they came to it.

Behind Angie and Luke, Leo walked with his hands shoved in his pockets, his eyes to the floor. As Angie and Luke stepped into the room with Wendy, Leo remained in the doorway, watching.

The room was decorated rather wonderfully, with a mahogany bookcase, a matching wardrobe, and a full-sized bed. The carpeting was lush and gray, and two armchairs in the center of the room were pointed toward the wall, where a fake fireplace was lined with red brick. A television hung on the wall over the fireplace, upon which, the nurse promised, Wendy would be able to watch all her favorite soap operas.

Angie and Luke guided Wendy into the armchair as the nurse continued to describe the daily routine of the residents at the care facility. Angie listened as intently as she could before dropping down to a squat next to her mother, taking her hand, and whispering, "We'll come to visit you all the time, Mom. You won't feel alone in the slightest."

The nurse overheard her and smiled. "She'll love your visits. But I can assure you, here in the memory wing, patient happiness is our utmost priority. We have social events and get-togethers all throughout the week. We do activities and crafts and have dances. Our patients become dear friends with one another. Like family. And on top of that, some of our residents actually find romance here within these walls."

Luke and Angie locked eyes. A smile played out across Luke's lips.

"Romance?" Luke asked.

The nurse nodded, clearly used to people thinking she was joking. "Our residents have lost huge portions of their lives from their memories. Why wouldn't we encourage them to live out the time they have left?"

Luke's smile dropped. "That makes so much sense."

"It really does," Angie breathed. "Thank you. Thank you for all the work you do here."

Suddenly, there was a soft knock outside the door of Wendy's room. Leo stepped to the side to reveal Hannah and baby Sophie, who lay angelically in a little carrier. Her large eyes tried to take stock of everything. Hollows lurked beneath

Hannah's eyes, proof that she hadn't slept much over the past few weeks. Still, she looked gorgeous and thrilled to be alive. Anyone could see that.

"Hi, honey!" Angie rushed to her feet. "I wasn't sure you'd make it."

Hannah stepped through the door, smiling. Wendy craned her head to catch sight of Hannah, whom she almost never remembered, no matter how hard Angie worked to remind her.

"Who's that?" Wendy asked, giving Hannah and her baby a smile.

"This is Hannah, Mom. Your granddaughter," Angie said, daring herself not to get sad all over again. There was nothing to be done about any of this. All they could do was press forward.

"And what little thing do you have there?" Wendy brightened. She looked like a much younger woman, optimistic.

Since Sophie was now three and a half weeks old, Hannah was accustomed to the world doting on her baby. She grinned and tenderly placed the carrier on the floor nearest to Wendy. Wendy splayed her hands out across her thighs, clearly wanting one thing and one thing only.

Hannah eyed her mother curiously, unsure. Angie gave Hannah a soft nod. She would watch out for Sophie, no matter what. Slowly, Hannah lifted Sophie from the carrier and placed her delicately in Wendy's arms.

Wendy's eyes softened. She was utterly captivated, her lips parted as she locked eyes with this gorgeous creature, her great-granddaughter. Angie's heart pounded as she watched this image. It wouldn't be so long before her mother left the world forever. It was miraculous, really, that Wendy and Sophie had been allowed this moment at all.

"How old is she?" Wendy asked.

"Twenty-four days," Hannah said. Recently, Angie and Hannah had grown sorrowful over the fact that soon, they would have to transition from saying "days old" to "months old."

"Twenty-four days," Wendy repeated. "How about that."

Another moment of silence. Sophie kicked her feet around and gurgled at her great-grandmother.

"She's talking to you," Hannah explained to Wendy.

"Oh, dear." Wendy shook her head. "I only wish I could understand what she's saying."

Suddenly, tears spilled down Wendy's cheeks. Her shoulders shuddered as a sob broke. Hannah took her baby into her arms and lifted her against her, watching as Wendy's first sob transformed into something animalistic and tragic. Angie dropped down and wrapped her arms around her mother.

But although her mother couldn't explain herself, Angie felt she understood, regardless. Probably, the last time Wendy had held a little girl in her arms, she'd had to give her away. Angie had lived a remarkable life after that, one that she was grateful for. But all the while, Wendy's arms had probably felt so empty.

Luke, Leo, Hannah, Angie, and baby Sophie stayed in Wendy's room for the rest of the visiting hours until the nurse returned to tell them that it was nearly time for lunch. One after another, they kissed Wendy on the cheek and said their goodbyes. Before long, they stood in the breeze of the parking lot, scuffing their shoes against the pavement, unsure of what to say.

"She seems good," Leo finished. "And the place is really spectacular. Far better than anything we could have afforded down in Boston." He coughed once, then added, "Thank you again for your help."

Angie nodded and raised her arms to hug her older brother. "Thank you for bringing her up here. Remember. Don't be a stranger. You're welcome up here any time."

"Any time," Luke echoed, hugging him just after Angie.

Luke, Angie, and Hannah stood in a line, waving until Leo drove his rental out of sight. For a long time, there was no sound, save for the rush of automobiles on the nearest highway.

And then, out of nowhere, Hannah said, "I'm starving."

"Me too," Luke said with a laugh. "Think we can hit up Snow's party a little early?"

"God, I hope so," Hannah said. "Abby said she's already there, setting up the cameras. No word on the pre-party snack situation, though. Abby's more motivated than I am."

"I'd argue that she didn't give birth twenty-four days ago," Angie countered.

"You're right. She doesn't know what it means to be so ravenous from breastfeeding," Hannah agreed.

"Or so ravenous from being a dude in his forties who never lost his sweet tooth," Luke countered.

Angie and Hannah groaned and laughed at once.

"Then let's hit the road." Angie grabbed her keys from her pocket and jangled them.

"Last one there is a rotten egg!" Luke cried, leaping toward his truck.

* * *

Apparently, that August party at the Snow Mansion was something of an anomaly. Prior to the Harvey Sisters' arrival to Bar Harbor, Evan Snow had been regarded as heinous and borderline evil, the sort of man who did anything for a buck and tore through anyone who got in his way.

But against all odds, Evan Snow had fallen in love with Nicole Harvey, the second-oldest Harvey Sister. With that, he'd connected with the people of Bar Harbor, assisted in the arrest of Brittany Keating's ex-husband, donated money to the Keating Inn and Acadia Eatery, and assisted with several Bar Harbor charity functions. He'd even thrown his brother under the bus for his own terrible crimes, coming out on top as a "reformed Snow Brother."

It was important to remember, of course, that Evan's wife had died in a car accident and left him broken-hearted and a shell of his previous self. It was said, then, that Nicole had brought him back to life again.

That August, Maddy Snow, Evan's youngest daughter, planned to move abroad for a semester. The Snow Party served as a part-going-away party and a part-end-of-summer party. As August dwindled away, everyone on Mount Desert Island felt the sharp sting of approaching autumn. At night, there was a real chill in the air.

Angie parked the car in the Snow driveway. Abby hustled out with a camera lifted to her eyes. As Hannah lifted Sophie from the car and carried her, Abby took a number of photographs, crying, "Look at them! Mother and baby."

Hannah stuck out her tongue at the camera. Abby laughed and dropped the camera against her chest before trying her best to both swallow Hannah in a hug and not irritate her hold on Sophie.

"I've missed you, my business partner," Abby said.

Hannah laughed. "I genuinely thought I'd be ready to work a couple of weeks ago. That was optimistic, to say the least."

"But you feel okay to snap some photos tonight?" Abby asked. "Evan agreed to our rate. Didn't even ask for friends and family discount."

"Fantastic," Hannah said. "What's our focus?"

"Maddy and her friends, for one," Abby explained. "This is their last hurrah before they leave Bar Harbor for good."

"Okay. Rich teenagers having the time of their lives. Check," Hannah said. "What else?"

"He said to just take in the ambiance of the party," Abby explained. "Evan wants to share the photographs with all of Bar Harbor. He wants to unite the town a little bit." She bent her head to whisper, "I mean, he's still trying to repair his terrible reputation. This party will do wonders for him."

"It really will," Hannah said with a nod.

Angie followed Hannah and Abby through the gate to discover Heather, Nicole, and Casey, already gathered around a tall table, sipping cocktails. A beautiful August sun purred over them, highlighting their beautiful sunglasses and the fluttering fabric of their summer dresses. For the first time in a long time, Angie didn't feel that familiar stab of jealousy upon first glance. Perhaps she liked her life too much these days to make stupid comparisons.

"There she is!" Heather rushed forward to hug Angie first. "I heard that you're performing for us tonight?"

"Ah. Yeah." Angie strung a curl behind her ear. "I'm a little embarrassed."

"Your whole jazz band?" Casey asked.

"Not quite," Angie explained. "A few of them were on vacation this week. But..."

"But the handsome drummer and my mom have cooked up their own little performance," Hannah interjected, wearing a silly grin.

"A handsome drummer?" Heather's eyes glittered. "Why is this the first time I'm hearing about this?"

Angie waved a hand, searching for the right words. But, as though the universe itself was up to its own tricks again, a deep and nourishing voice called her name from behind her. Angie turned to find Paul, his familiar drumsticks in his back pocket.

"Oh my God," Casey muttered under her breath. "Is that your handsome drummer?"

Angie's heart flipped over. Their eyes connected, and for a little while, it seemed as though the rest of the wild world around them faded away. It had been five days since they'd finally, finally shared their first kiss in the shadows of the practice room. Both had ached with it, knowing it would happen when it happened. When it finally did, Angie had walked home with her heart in her throat, forgetting that she'd driven there. She'd had to walk back the next day to grab her car.

Angie introduced Paul, sounding girlish and strange. Everyone shook his hand and greeted him warmly. Casey disappeared and returned with a beer, placing it in his hand. She reported that Evan and Maddy were inside, having the first of what would probably be "several" spats that afternoon.

"They love each other to bits," Nicole explained. "But they just can't find a way to get along."

Casey groaned. "I'm just grateful my kids aren't teenagers anymore."

Hannah peered into Sophie's carrier, where the little girl now slept angelically. "She'll never give me a hard time. I just know it."

"Yeah. Talk to us in sixteen years," Casey returned.

The conversation trickled on. Guests from around Bar Harbor arrived, grabbing drinks from the bar area, and enjoying light snacks like garlic bread and crab puffs. Hannah left Sophie's carrier with Angie and disappeared with Abby to begin taking photographs. Already, they were hard at work, hunting for the perfect angles and the iconic moments— ones that people wanted to remember after the night was over.

And eventually, just as ever, the conversation found its way back to the hostage situation. Even weeks later, nobody quite knew what to say about it. But this time, apparently, Paul had some fresh information directly from the Bar Harbor Police Station.

"I told you already that the bank robbers were slated to lose everything," Paul began. "The bank had denied the oldest one a loan, and he was angry and scared and willing to do anything to stay afloat."

Angie grimaced, dropping her eyes to the table. "You did."

"Gosh, that's awful," Nicole breathed.

"But..." Paul's eyes burrowed into Angie's.

"What is it?" Angie asked, suddenly terrified.

"Well. I recently found out that the man in charge of the bank chain that denied the men their loans was Carter Baxter," Paul continued.

Angie furrowed her brow for a minute, unsure if she understood. "Baxter? You mean..."

Paul nodded. His fingers crept through Angie's, cradling her hand. He then explained to the rest of the party.

"A few weeks ago, Angie and I performed at a terribly expensive wedding outside of Portland. I've never seen anything so ornate," he began. "It's one of those coincidences, learning that the father of the groom— the man who paid for that wedding— was the man responsible for the bank robbers' losing their livelihoods. It's a horrible contrast, isn't it? Those men will probably go to prison for the rest of their lives. And the man in charge of the bank will eat caviar and drink champagne and never think of those men again."

Angie's stomach twisted with a strange mix of rage and sorrow. None of the Harvey Sisters knew what to say.

Finally, Angie found the strength.

"It should never have happened that way," she breathed. "Nobody should have to suffer so much just to put food on the table for their families. Nobody should have to threaten people just to figure out a way to survive."

Paul's grip tightened on her hand. One after another, Heather, Casey, and Nicole lifted their drinks and nodded.

But could they ever fully understand what Angie and Hannah had gone through that year? Angie wasn't sure.

She supposed, though, that it didn't matter. Everyone carried their own unique baggage, their own horrific stories, and their own private pains. Angie and Hannah had burrowed their way to the center of the earth and, somehow, come out on the other side, bathed in sunlight.

When Hannah arrived back, flipping through her two hundred and fifty-two photographs, already eyeing the best ones, Evan approached to ask Angie and Paul to begin their set. Angie dropped a kiss on Hannah's cheek before she disappeared into the shadows of the corner, where Paul had set up the drum set and the keyboard earlier that morning.

With Angie's fingers hovering over the keyboard and Paul stationed on his drum set, Angie's heart shimmered with expectation, with vitality, with hope. For this set, Paul and Angie had agreed to do what they did best— making things up as they went along, improvising, and creating brand-new songs for a live audience. Through this form of music-making, Angie could feel the budding love between the two of them. She could sense the gorgeous future they would one day create.

Just then, they were only a few weeks into their journey.

How lucky they were that they had the rest of their lives.

Paul raised his drumsticks a half-inch from the skin of the drum. His eyes locked with Angie's. This time, he didn't even have to count down. There was a sudden twitch of his shoulders, and suddenly, the two of them were off to the races— creating a song that had never been heard.

It was pure magic and uniquely theirs. Perhaps nobody would ever truly understand it the way they did. And that, Angie knew, was the greatest gift of all.

Coming Next

Coming Next in the Bar Harbor Series

Pre order A New Light

Other Books by Katie

The Vineyard Sunset Series

Secrets of Mackinac Island Series

Sisters of Edgartown Series

A Katama Bay Series

A Mount Desert Island Series

A Nantucket Sunset Series

Connect with Katie Winters

BookBub
Facebook
Newsletter

To receive exclusive updates from Katie Winters please sign up to be on her Newsletter!
CLICK HERE TO SUBSCRIBE